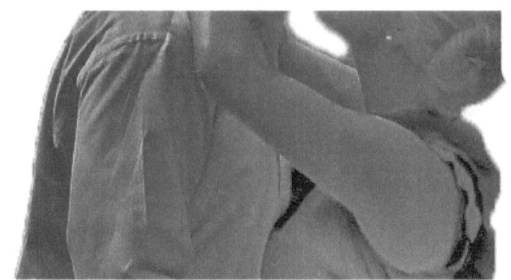

FABRICATIONS

Dᴀᴠɪᴅ R. Sʟᴀᴠɪᴛᴛ

Aɴᴀᴘʜᴏʀᴀ Lɪᴛᴇʀᴀʀʏ Pʀᴇss

Aᴛʟᴀɴᴛᴀ, GᴇᴏʀGɪᴀ

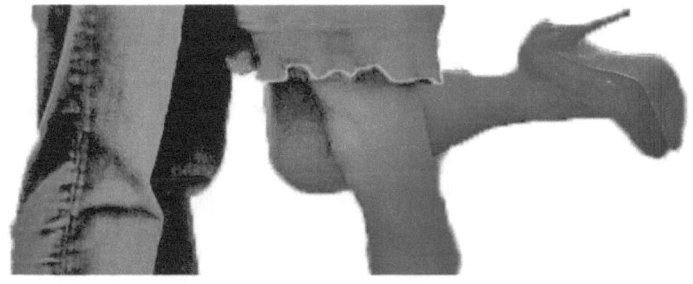

ANAPHORA LITERARY PRESS
1803 Treehills Parkway
Stone Mountain, GA 30088
http://anaphoraliterary.com

Book design by Anna Faktorovich, Ph.D.

Published in 2015 by Anaphora Literary Press

Fabrications
David R. Slavitt—1st edition.

ISBN-13: 978-1-68114-085-8
ISBN-10: 1-68114-085-3
EBook ISBN: 978-1-681140-86-5

Library of Congress Control Number: 2015904378

FABRICATIONS

_____

DAVID R. SLAVITT

In the real world, death is eternal; in fiction it is perpetual.

—Marion Rombauer

For Elena and Yoni

I

It is ten minutes to eleven.

True as I write this, in a minute it won't be. And if there are readers for whatever this is, it will be fiction for them, unless they want to check their watches and start reading at 10:49:59 so that it will be true for them, too. For a minute at least. Then it will be history, in which it is also difficult to believe, for that, too is a story. Really (as we say so casually) can we expect more than a minute's truth in this mutable and duplicitous world? We have no idea what is happening and hardly even know who we are, so we make up plausible stories that are, like Ptolemaic astronomy, both accurate (nearly) and wacky (entirely). In most moments of conversation, my fiction of myself is talking to yours. No, this is not satisfactory, but there is no complaint department and neither you nor I can claim to be still under warranty. In any discourse, there is wiggle room that may be the only freedom we have. For instance, I said "watches," but for many it will be "cell phones." Does that make a difference? No. But of course it does. It is now five minutes to eleven. But I can raise the bar. And add "AM." Or even higher and say "Monday."

Less and less "true." More and more "fictional."

Has no one ever thought to explain to librarians, bookstore owners, and children that there is no "non-fiction"?

✳

Decisions. Should we be in the past tense or the present? [If the tense is past, then we can relax. And don't forget to breathe!] That is not a difficult question because, as we have agreed, there is, at best, a notional present. Then turns instantly into now which immediately morphs back into then. It's giddying. And it rushes by too quickly for any of us to get a good look. An instant's impression and we testify, under oath sometimes, that this is what happened. Eyewitness testimony is notoriously unreliable. Unless the culprit was a one-legged dwarf with a long red beard, the witness is probably making it up. That blur of time is fascinating to children. What is destiny and what is random? Was it destined for me to raise my right arm? Or was it destiny for me to ask the question and then not raise my arm? Grown-ups don't bother themselves about these abstruse problems. To do so would be unintelligent (but oddly only intelligent people can be stupid).

Meanwhile, should we be in the first person or third? Neither makes any sense. If I have only an imprecise notion of who I am, any character I propose will be even less self-aware than me (or, rather, his or her self-awareness will be even less accurate than mine.) Fourth person? (I wish.) From the sixth dimension? (Sure, why not?) And the narrator can be Schrödinger's cat, dead and alive. Fortunately, there was no cat. There was no box. It was a *Gedankenexperiment*, which is, whether or not Herr Doktor Professor Schrödinger would have admitted it, a kind of fiction. And we are allowed to imagine this putative cat thinking about the physicist, who is always (or sometimes, or never) opening lid of his box and peering in.

Ridiculee, ridiculah, ridiculous--but life is, mostly. As novels are, or should be, if they are to have any relevance to the world beyond the biding of their bindings. Let us imagine a character (or, first, let us imagine an "us," which is already a considerable feat). He is based in part on a friend of mine, dead now but lively enough when he was alive. And therefore, in some sense, lively still. There is, in other words, some truth to this—although that doesn't count for anything. "The truth is stranger and a thousand times more thrilling than fiction." *True Comics* used to proclaim that on its covers, but I was never sure that it was true. (Wouldn't it be great if it were and literary critics referred to it as an authority? An idea is not necessarily invalidated by its source. One could cite as a reference in monographs "Double Bubble Facts" with a date maybe. It would enliven scholarly indices to have such a citation tucked among the listings for Merleau-Ponty, Husserl, and Lukács.)

The sad fact is that a good many teachers of English have abandoned literature and now criticize reality, pointing out that slavery was a bad thing. (Really?) And that women have had a tough time of it for the past couple of thousand years. (No kidding!) It's easier to attract the students who dislike dragging their eyeballs across lines of print.

But back to my dead friend. I knew him, I guess, for sixty years, give or take. Abner, let's call him. A nice, solid, biblical name—he was Saul's cousin and a general. The initial is accurate; the other letters are invented, which feels about right because that's what happens to characters in novels who are, more often than not, *salades composées*. I still remember our first significant encounter, in front of a prep school dorm where he lived in the room across the hall from mine. I returned from class one afternoon to find that he had removed all the light bulbs from their fixtures and replaced them with blue ones. When I asked him why, he told me he wanted it to look like the Kiss Room at El Borracho.

I think of him as an F. Scott Fitzgerald character, born a generation too late.

Not Gatsby, but maybe but Wolfsheim, from whose point of view there might well be another, even more interesting novel. Wolfsheim is *infra dignitatem* because he is Jewish and a bootlegger. So he's a little like Joe Kennedy or rather say one of the Bronfmans (Bronfmen?). Jews and booze are no longer inherently disgraceful. What makes Wolfsheim attractive is that he lacks Gatsby's nutty pretension and ambition. He's a realist, whose take on the narrative would be better informed and more perceptive than Nick Carraway's. For all we know, Gatsby may be Jewish himself. His background is mysterious. And Carraway? Those are the seeds on the crusts of Jewish rye bread, with which with even goyish Midwesterners would have been familiar.

Let us suppose that Wolfsheim's father had been a guest at Trotsky's bar mitzvah. Give him a little stature (Wolfsheim, not Trotsky). The tradition in novels is that Jews, except for Daniel Deronda, are sinister. That sinister note in Gatsby's story is what makes it interesting. No? Nu?

But we were at the El Borracho, I think. I should point out that Abner and I were both sixteen. Nightclubs? I had not been allowed to travel into New York City alone until I was fourteen or so. (A dangerous place, my parents thought, even though there were obviously children who managed somehow to grow up there.) You can perhaps imagine my admiration of the wackiness of both his gesture and its explanation. I wished I had it in me to do such things. I didn't want actually to do them so much as be capable of them. A diffident ambition, but one must not be too cowardly to admit his cowardice--at least to himself.

In any event, wanting has nothing whatever to do with what happens.

❊

We both imagined that we would write, which is rather different from wanting to be writers—a dismal and often heart-breaking occupation about which neither of us knew a thing at the time. We had read books but, never having met a living author, we were left to imagine whatever we could. There was perhaps a glamorous squalor to it, like Rodolfo's in *La Bohème*, but that was too silly to frighten us. In any event, Paris was not real. Neither was France or, for that matter, Europe. Our notion of being writers was rather a means by which we could be both participants and observers in our limited lives. It was a self-consciousness we shared that can be an enlivening quality in teen-agers. I was a conventionally bookish kid. He was more diverse. The records he played, for instance, were not just of classical music but extended in range to include jazz and Broadway show tunes as well as Charles Trenet, Edith Piaf and...Yma Sumac, "the Voice of the Xtabay!" Remember her? She was a Peruvian soprano with a range of many octaves. If Rima, the bird girl, could have sung, she would have sounded like Sumac. The music was strange to my ears with its extravagant runs and staccato hoots that made me feel (yet again) like the country mouse, intimidated by the sophistication of his city cousin. [Actually, it's Rima the jungle girl I was trying to think of, the character in *Green Mansions*; the bird girl is in a Rona Jaffe story. It is an excusable confusion.)

I came to realize that, like Gatsby's glitter, Abner's was to some degree feigned. He wasn't from New York or the Virginia horse country or the Eastern Shore of Maryland but from Texas. (Fitzgerald was from Minnesota, which doesn't glitter much either.) I thought of Texas, then, and still do, mostly, as a Never-never-land of ludicrous excess. How to explain this? It wasn't condescension on my part. (I could never have presumed to condescend to Abner) but just exotic. In Dallas some years ago, I was taken to dinner at Brennan's—a branch of the one in New Orleans. There was a threesome at a table near ours, two blue-haired ladies and an old guy with a large turquoise bolo around his neck. They were celebrating something or other and he ordered crêpes Suzette for desert. When the waiter brought over the cart and started to prepare it, the geezer said to one of the women, "Looka there, Mama, he's fryin' orange peels," which, for me, is that state's motto. (For Texans, it's "Friendship," which isn't very exciting, even if the word is a translation of the Caddo word, "teyshas," which means friendship and probably gives the state its name.) For an instant, as the dramatic flames arose from the crêpes pan, I thought of Abner and realized how much he must have been carrying in his luggage.

That Brennan's dinner must have been more than forty years ago. But odd bits like that surface now and then. The mind--an old man's mind, anyway--is like Pearl Harbor, where you stare at the water, waiting for a blob of oil to surface from the Arizona. They come up from the submerged hulk every twenty to thirty seconds. People say that it's the sunken ship weeping. Fine, if that comforts them, but it would be weeping upward, which is odd. I think of the phenomenon as emblematic of an old man's memory. You ask yourself a question, often about a name, and the answer eludes you. You could look it up, of course but, if the subject isn't important, it can be pleasing just to wait. (Name the five Stooges!) More often than not it will, without any cue, surface. (Curly-Joe!) The coy brain cells are demonstrating that they can still work, if they feel like it. But the process often takes longer than thirty seconds.

Texas. The thought of its ebullient extravagance brings Abner's parents to mind. Even before the business with the blue lights, I had met them at the beginning of the year in front of the dorm when they brought Abner up to school in their huge, white Lincoln. His father was maybe 6' 4" and his mother of normal height but putting on weight. Aggressively blonde. The father's name was also Abner; his mother's was Lurlene, and I have never met another woman with that name. Both of them spoke in a parody of a Texas accent, in which I remember one of them saying, "Bye, then, Bitsy, and good luck to ya."

That was the instant when our friendship began. Abner looked around in dismay. I was the only one close enough to have heard. He didn't say anything. More important, I didn't say anything, then or ever. I realized in that instant that I had it in my power to ruin his life. The guy standing near Edmund Wilson who heard his parents say, "Goodbye, Bunny," when they dropped him off at the Hill School had not kept quiet so that, when he was a fat, old, eminent man, people were still calling him "Bunny." At that moment, I didn't know about Wilson's story, but I could figure out easily enough that Abner would prefer me to ignore what I had heard. After a few days, he began to trust me a little. If I hadn't told his secret to anyone by then there was at least a hope that I'd continue to keep my mouth discretely shut for the rest of the term—which was as far ahead as any of us could think. He was increasingly grateful, although he couldn't mention that. It became enough of a bond between us to support at least the beginning of a friendship.

I said he was the sophisticated one and he was. I wasn't exactly stupid though. He enjoyed dazzling me; other than that, we shared a refined sense of humor. He could be very funny. So could I in a drier way. Which meant we could stand each other's company and even sometimes enjoy it.

❖

I should perhaps correct a false impression. I was talking about Texas and mentioned Dallas, so that one might suppose Abner came from Dallas. Not hardly. Lubbock, which is one of those joke towns like Paris or Waco or Lovelady. These are figments. Not that Dallas, Houston, or Austin are plausible places, but I have been to all three of them and have to admit grudgingly that they exist. The others? Movie sets for gunfights with a livery stable, a barbershop, a hotel, and a saloon with spittoons between the barstools and those swinging double-doors. These days, there's probably a putt-putt track and a miniature golf course. Because it is so improbable, it would have been a likely place for Abner to have come from—a distant planet in some ways not unlike our own.

This isn't merely blather. What I'm suggesting—and it took me years to come to the realization—was that Abner had to invent himself, more than most youngsters from the northeast. In this, he was like one of his idols,

Cole Porter, who was born in Indiana. Peru, actually, and the stress is on the first syllable, which is, of course, long—as if the name were pee rue. And now that Cole has been mentioned, the question comes about Abner's sexuality, which I never thought to ask or even to wonder about back then, when the only way you could tell that someone was gay was that he was wearing mascara, which Abner didn't do. My guess now is that he was bisexual. Or, as they used to say at school, a quadrisexual, which is someone who will do anything with anyone for a quarter.

He had a picture of a girl in a leather frame on his bureau. Mary Lamb, he said her name was. Really! In Texas they do that kind of thing. The Lambs had a little Mary, right? Makes a hell of a birth announcement although it may provoke unwanted chuckles for the rest of the poor kid's life. A pretty, oval-faced girl with bouffant hair, which was the fashion back in the fifties. Not inconceivably, the frame came with the photograph in it, which would have appealed to Abner's sense of humor. But the photo did what it was supposed to do and served as a declaration that he was straight. Nobody thought of challenging that.

Now that it isn't any big deal, I can see that there were signs I might not have picked up as a teen-ager. The Broadway shows? The musical he wrote at school in our senior year, an impish work of which I only remember a couple of lines:

Hark, hark, the lark,
we are going to the park
to see the whippoorwill and chickadee.
It is such great fun
in the morning sun
      to spy upon the wee pee wee.

Abner danced around the stage while a quite good tenor sang this, and what I still remember was that he had glitter on his eyelids. (Not quite mascara but close.)

Also, he never married, which is another hint, although I didn't have that information back then. But he had a Mary Lamb, who might or might not have been a... "beard" is it? I plead innocence or maybe just ignorance. There were masters who disappeared abruptly during the middle of a term and the rumors that went around were that they were chicken hawks who had finally been caught cruising the back streets of Lawrence or Lowell or, worse, preying on the students. Often, these were the best teachers, which stands to reason. Secondary school teaching is not all that demanding intellectually, so teachers do better at it if they're interested in the students—however that interest may manifest itself.

I was never hit on. Or approached. I still haven't been. I assume that I'm lacking in whatever homosexuals find attractive, although this hasn't been a great concern of mine. I mention all this only because it is relevant to the curious story of Abner's life. Not crucial, I think, but still worth mentioning.

Only lately have I begun to wonder whether the gayness might have been a refuge from the Jewishness. Or from his Texas roots. Remember how James Baldwin morphed from being a black man who happened to be gay to a gay man who happened to be black? Now that gays are liberated and even can get married, they don't have any special character, but back then, when they were illegal, they had a certain panache. Like Oscar Wilde, maybe, or Auden. In literary terms, the distinction is clear between the undershirt-and-beer-can realists, and the Truman Capote and Gore Vidal exquisites, the academic doubts about Hemingway notwithstanding. It wasn't just a sexual preference (or destiny) but a stylistic assertion. If one weren't gay, he might well be "posing as a somdomite" (to use the Marquis of Queensbury's sic phrase). What one did in bed didn't (and doesn't) matter so much as what one did at the desk. Jews must endure the slurs of anti-Semites; queers have to put up with the anger (and fears) of boors and fools, which is a tougher battle.

After we graduated, we went on to the same university where we remained friends. We were in different residential colleges but had lunch together every couple of weeks. We had, I think, only one class together, a seminar on the poetry of George Herbert. After class, more often than not, we'd have coffee and talk about poetry, life and even, sometimes, George Herbert. I remember that Abner had figured out that his religious poems were love poems in disguise, all about yearning for acceptance of one kind or another. The teacher had not made this comparison in his discussions and I'm pretty sure Abner had thought it up on his own.

What he saw about me was my reliable naiveté or say my wide-eyed reaction to some of his stories. He and a group of friends had gone to the Copacabana, although that's not what one said. "*J'y vais*," was enough. I am going "there." I don't know how many of them there were, but after Abner picked up the check for the whole crowd he worried about what his parents would say. I couldn't even imagine my parents' reaction to a nightclub bill of four thousand nineteen-fifties dollars. I mean, you could buy a car for that!

It didn't occur to me to ask why he hadn't invited me. I wasn't that kind of person. I didn't go "there." I stayed on campus, reading assigned texts. Some of us did that from time to time, although it wasn't cool ever to be seen working.

Whenever we talked about books, my contributions were mostly about books that had been assigned. I hardly ever read current fiction, but that was Abner's main interest. I didn't think of these as serious, but he paid attention to them in the same way that people read newspapers, to see what is going on here and now. (He was right, of course, but I only came to understand that later on.)

The attention I paid to course work didn't leave me much time. Then too, that's what I had been trained to do by my ambitious parents-- to "apply myself," as my father used to say. Abner's folks, although it is easy enough to make fun of them, were more relaxed and allowed their Bitsy a little leeway for recreation and diversion. He chafed much more than I at the constraints of prep school life; at college, he was more at home. (I remember going out for a cup of coffee a little after ten on my first evening there. No "sign-outs," no curfews. No rules. I could just walk out of my room, out of the dorm, and along the streets delighting in this first taste of freedom. I never mentioned this to Abner. It was a clearer admission than I wanted to make of how sheltered my existence had been until that moment. This was hardly Abner's problem.

What I remember with particular vividness is a remark Abner made during that lazy week between our final exams and commencement. "What we've gotta do," he said, in that lazy, Texan drawl that was somewhere between a mutter and a growl, "is change our names and enroll at Princeton. And this time, we'll do it right!"

It has the casual *profondeur* of many of his comments. One cannot change the past, redo it, or correct it. It's there, as solid as the Gothic and Georgian buildings we'd been living in for four years.

I'm afraid those buildings, mildly silly when they were erected, have become increasingly mocking and accusatory. They were supposed to suggest an older era in which young men went off for a few years of *Studentenleben* to study, drink, contemplate the world, and discover who they were, much has they had been doing since early renaissance times. Now, the youngsters— men and women—are studying economics, computer programming, applied mathematics, and such practical subjects that are as un-Gothic as they can be. "The Virgin" has given way to "the dynamo," and Henry Adams' discomfort is now shared among many of us but there is nothing to be done. Our clocks are atomic now (cesium, I think) and cannot be set back.

To be fair about it, though, the economy was better in the fifties, and we could study whatever amused us, which is the right way to go about it. I can't remember who said it, maybe the university president making a joke, but the idea of an education was to prepare you to live an interesting life, even if you happen to be the beneficiary of a million-dollar trust fund. (A million was a lot, back then.) The point of the joke was that, whatever you wanted to do, you'd do it better with a mind that wasn't altogether unfurnished. If you wanted to make money, fine, but then when you came to spend it—on art, travel, philanthropy, or whatever—you'd be better equipped to do it well. What the president didn't have to say was, "Relax. Yalies don't starve."

Abner and I both majored in English, mostly because it was easy. We already knew how to read and write (not all entering freshmen did) and we liked poetry and novels and plays, realizing that they had been written mostly to entertain. We were willing to be entertained and even curious about how some of these things worked, so that when we came to try to produce something on our own, we might have some clue as to how to go about it. What we didn't realize was that twenty-year-olds haven't lived and don't know anything yet. But that is a defect that cures itself. We didn't read each other's essays, but I would often see his work in the literary magazine and he'd see mine I thought of him, I confess, as talented but something of a lightweight—not that there's anything wrong with that. Max Beerbohm? Ronald Firbank?

Surprisingly, he was the first to publish a novel, *Is It Morning Already?* It was just a couple of years after we graduated and was more or less an updated version of *This Side of Paradise*, or so the publishers claimed. Perhaps that was what they thought and how they persuaded themselves that it might be promotable and could even make money. They bestirred themselves, which they seldom do for first novels. They advertised it. There were a couple of magazine and newspaper articles about him. But even so, the book didn't sell all that many copies (neither did *This Side of Paradise*, for that matter, or not in the first year).

I suppose I must have been jealous but I was also pleased for him and impressed (surprised?) that he had the *Sitzfleisch* to produce a whole book. And the need. We write because, for one reason or another, we have to, and this was his way of defining himself and asserting to the world that his definition had some truth to it. The alternatives? He could have gone back to Texas, I suppose, or he could have hung around in New York and got some job with a magazine or an ad agency or maybe a television network. None of these is a mean ambition. But he was going to do it right. He had a little money. (His parents were generous to their Bitsy and proud of him for having graduated.) He had some time. It would be foolish not to use it.

Okay, fine. But then what? He was shrewd enough to realize that another novel right away might not be a good idea. The reading public is fickle and easily bored. More seriously, he thought he could let himself live a little and write about whatever happened.

The book had created just enough of a stir to attract the attention of a

Hollywood producer. He was only mildly interested in the book—which got optioned in one of those deals where most of the money was payable on the first day of shooting (which rarely happens). But the producer, Lou Levin, was interested in him and flew him out to LA to discuss ideas. Abner was delighted. And Levin, who was clever (aren't they all?), pitched the not very farfetched notion of a young kid who gets out of college, has a little money, and decides to go and bum around in France for a while. Paris? St. Tropez? Just hang out and see what happens. Then we'll talk.

Incredible? I thought so at the time, but I have learned a little since then. For some Hollywood producers, the path to success meant never hiring anyone who needed the job. (I've heard that said in so many words.) The other way to go is with small bets on long shots. Possibly Levin thought he might eventually get a screenplay out of Abner. Or something that could be made into one. And if not? There were always other projects. The worst case was that he could write off Abner's trip and let the kid have a good time in France for a few months. (I assume that Levin was gay and found Abner attractive.). And then, for all I know, Levin might have had some weird kind of cost-plus arrangement with a studio so that for every dollar he spent, he got a dollar and a quarter back. It can happen. Abner, I'm sure, would not have troubled himself about how and why. He just ate the dinner, took the money, and promised Levin that he'd be in touch--as I would have done if I'd had the chance.

He flew back to New York, put his things in storage, and booked passage on the Queen Mary. We had a bon voyage lunch at a wonderful smorgasbord that doesn't exist anymore (The Stockholm, maybe?) because one could feast grandly for a modest amount of money. Not just herring, but shrimp and lobster halves, and roast beef, and maybe twenty different kinds of salad. It wasn't a place he knew and he was delighted with it. We toasted each other with aquavit. But he'd have been just as delighted at the Automat. I remember it as the happiest moment we ever spent together. His eyes were bright. He spoke rather more rapidly than usual. It was as if he were high but without the drugs. He was on his way to Europe to loll in the sun and amuse himself until some idea crossed his mind that was worth writing down, ideally on a nightclub napkin. "What kind of luck is this?" he asked. I said it was splendid, but I had the sense that he didn't attribute it all to luck. He was just being polite, not wanting to strut too much or seem to be boasting. He thought, I have no doubt, that the luck was part of the package and went with the talent. To some extent, he thought the talent deserved it. Cuckoo Calvinism, you could call it. He never said so, but I knew him well enough to hear that descant to the matter-of-fact tone of his talk about where he might go and what he might do over there.

I have only a vague notion of his life during those two years. We exchanged letters or post cards but only sporadically, because, sooner or later, we'd meet up and could catch each other up. In one of the letters he informed me that he sometimes visited Prince Yusupov's house in the Marais. How he got invited to the prince's parties, he didn't say and I can't imagine, but he was an ornament, an attractive young American who had published a novel . . . Why not? There would be drinks, vodka of course, and because Yusupov was a prince, when he drank everyone else had to drink. And he drank a lot. By the time dinner was served, only a few guests could walk downstairs to the dining room without clutching the handrails and staggering a little. Dinner—for fourteen—was invariably a stewed chicken, a little of which went a very long way because everyone was too far gone to eat much. Food was expensive, after all, but the vodka was cheap because the prince had a still up on the roof where he produced his own. After dinner, they would all go up to the top floor, some on hands and knees on the staircases, and someone played the pipe organ while the prince flipped the pages of "the book," which was a catalogue of the wedding presents he and the princess had received. It looked more or less like a catalogue from Van Cleef and Arpels, except that here and there a stone or an entire piece was X'ed out with a grease pencil, those being ones he'd had to sell to keep up his peculiar establishment.

True? I assume so. He might have embroidered some, but it would have been strenuous even for Abner to make all of it up. But who could invent a pipe organ? Sophistication I grant him, but princely extravagance, I think, would have been a bit beyond him. And he wasn't a student of architecture, so that his description of the house that was larger and larger the higher it went was persuasive to me. Just as interesting, but perhaps too good to be true was his offhand remark that he lived for some months over there, after the money ran out, on elderly countesses and hors d'oeuvres. (Did the adjective apply to the hors d'oeuvres, too?) On the other hand, some of the time must have been fun. He alluded once to his having danced with Brigitte Bardot at L'Esquinade in St. Tropez. He was a very good dancer. And she? It didn't much matter, did it?

❖

Letters? I suppose I should explain. This was before email and back when long-distance telephone calls cost a lot more than they do these days. But beyond that, Abner and I got into the habit of exchanging written letters early on. Neither of us ever said this explicitly, but I am sure he shared my hope that one or, preferably, both of us might get famous and that our correspondence, filed away in some library, would be of interest to scholars. It's a low-grade immortality, I suppose. We also liked the *arrière garde* affectation.

Neither of us wrote with goose quills on hand-laid paper or sealed our letters with wax, but we didn't need those appurtenances.

Eventually, he came home. Desperate enough to admit that this adventure of his wasn't going anywhere and wasn't even that much fun anymore, he wired home. His parents helped him out, even though they had both taken a dim view of his "gallivanting.") It was only on the plane when he was reading a used paperback he'd bought for the flight--*Nicholas and Alexandra* by Robert Massie--that he discovered at last who Prince Felix Felixovich Yusupov was--the fellow who had killed Rasputin. Poisoned him with enough cyanide to kill a horse, and then shot him (twice), and then wrapped him in a rug and drowned him in the Neva. I mention this here not to put Abner down but to demonstrate the naivety that went along with his spotty sophistication in a combination that was a curious part of his charm.

So, back to Lubbock. His father I think had died about then and he stayed there with Lurlene in the house in which he'd grown up--until he couldn't stand it anymore. Exactly what precipitated his move to California, I'm not sure—not that there needs to be much explanation for putting Lubbock in one's rearview mirror. It was a place where he was Bitsy again, treated like a kid and, for all I know, being told when to go to bed.

"Live Love Lubbock" They have posters for sale with that motto and various Lubbockian scenes. What absurdist novelist (on what medications) could dream up their slogan: "the sports capital of West Texas"? I imagine they must have a minor league baseball team. If not, we can dream one up for them. The Lubbock Bullocks? (No, there'd be jokes about ballocks.) The Lions? (Trite.) The Leopards sounds too much like lepers. The Cheetahs? (Cheaters.) Or the Ring-tailed Lemurs? I like that, but it'd be a hard sell. The Lummoxes? (Great!) Or the Lummoxen? (Even better.) It isn't the hopelessness but the relentless cheer of the citizens that I imagine he found intolerable. As they pass each other in the streets, spurs clinking chunka-chunk, they exchange greetings: "Hiya!" "Howdy." "How's yourself?" "Hihi!" If it were the peculiar side effect of something in the water, it would be amusing, but they are unimpaired and altogether sincere. And insufferable. What's really frightening is the idea that it might be catching. You, too, could become one of them. "Hi, there!" "Hi back!" And touching the brim of your Stetson as we've learned to do in all those movies. Of course he left. (I wonder if James Arness, out of makeup and costume, continued to touch the brim of his hat, or Marshall Dillon's, as he strolled along the streets of Beverly Hills. And did he think if not actually say, "Howdy"?)

Did you know that James Arness's brother was Peter Graves? (Details like this are supposed to give fiction a certain verisimilitude.)

He settled, eventually in Malibu. Abner, I mean, not Arness or Graves, where he sublet the only slum I've ever heard of in that enclave of extravagance. My vague memory is that he'd sent a treatment of a movie—a couple of years late, but even so—to Levin, who invited him to come out to talk about it. Reasonable people would suppose that the pronoun had an antecedent, which should have been the treatment, but producer talk is neither strictly grammatical nor informative nor even representational. "It" was anything Levin wanted it to be, including the idea of Abner's doing scut work for him on the cheap. (Abner didn't have an agent, wasn't a member of the Writers' Guild, and had no idea what the going rates were for various kinds of jobs. He hadn't the least idea how the industry functioned. The studio system had collapsed not long before, and producers, now on their own, were contriving fictive deals that kept them occupied and sometimes brought in a few real dollars. Let us suppose that Levin bought the rights to a newly published novel. $200,000? Why not? It turns out that only $2,000 is payable up front for a two year option, the rest is pure fantasy, being due on the first day of shooting, which is unlikely ever to happen. So Levin has this putative property. (A novel doesn't sound impressive, but now that it has turned into a "property" it's more substantial. Properties, as all businessmen know, are for buying and selling.) What the producer now has to do is to reduce the novel into something salable, which is to say arrange for a "short treatment." Who's going to read a whole goddamn novel, after all? You hire people to do that. Like Li'l Abner. You take him to lunch and you pay him two or three thousand dollars to read the book and write a ten-page summary. Then you take another producer to a more expensive lunch (that's another couple of hundred) and you sell him the treatment and the rights package for, say, ten grand. Packages are also businesslike. After expenses (the first two thousand, Abner's lunch and two thousand, and the lunch with the other producer), you come out ahead. Chicken feed? Well, sure, but as Frank Perdue figured out, you can live on chicken. If you do this kind of thing twice a month, it will tide you over until a real movie happens and manna falls out of the smoggy sky.

Had I been in Abner's place, which is to say unmarried and childless, I would probably have gone out there, too. It's an adventure and you can always come back to the real world. You don't need an exit visa. (It would have been worrisome for me that the ticket Levin sent was only one-way, but it would have seemed too petty to bicker about.) Abner shows up at Levin's showy office. Of course it was showy. This is show business in which, quite reasonably, most of what they do is for show. Big desk. Splashy abstract painting on the wall (you can rent these). Antique (or made to look like one) French wardrobe that had been fitted with shelves and that Levin used as a file cabinet. And lots of plants (also rented). Abner sits in one of the *bergères* that face the desk. And Levin gives his incoherent appraisal of "Under the Blue Umbrella," which is the name of Abner's screenplay. With the rhetoric removed, what he was saying was that it was a great idea but there was no idea there. That's probably when Abner should have left, gone back to the airport or even the bus terminal, and returned to Lubbock, where people may not be glamorous or even interesting but don't all talk mendacious nonsense.

It isn't entirely bad, though. Levin likes the idea that it prompted in his mind—a Beach Blanket Bingo kind of movie but set in France and more sophisticated. (By which he meant that it could show tits.) He suggested that they work on it together but, in the meanwhile, Abner would need something to live on. There was a book Levin had acquired. Could Abner read it and write a five- to-ten-page summary of it, for a couple of thousand bucks? Of course. Why not?

He finds himself a cheap garden apartment he can get month-to-month, puts his Olivetti on the desk, and is now a Hollywood writer, or almost.

Levin was a snake but could do a generous thing now and then, especially if it didn't cost him anything. He spread the word around that Abner was good for this kind of work and wasn't a member of The Writer's Guild of America, West. This made him attractive to other cheapskate producers with other properties and packages. It soon grew into a marginal but steady business. The only danger was of his getting caught by the Guild but that would happen only if one of these projects had gone somewhere, not all the way to a green light maybe but far enough to be noticed. And the penalty would have been his having to pay back dues, but in that event he'd have money and could afford it.

At that age, one doesn't question how things turn out or what else one might have done. Otherwise is a country for old men. Years later, talking about his initiation into the treatment game, he said that he'd never intended to make a steady thing of it, but that was what had happened. He was half persuaded that it must have been fate. His ambition and his sense self-worth that comes from having talent (even a little) told him that everything would work out somehow. (As they did for so many other writers who went out there to get chewed up and spat out?) Outside of work, which was hardly strenuous, the existence was comfortable and amusing, rather like bumming around in France. Bars, nightclubs, beaches, occasional games of tennis on somebody's backyard court, and places to eat where he could look out at the water. The treatments were like papers for an English class but without the thinking. (Producers dislike thinking and most of them are allergic to it.)

So there he is for a matter of months that blur by like the palm trees along the boulevards when you're driving. They stretch into years and then, at some point, he meets Nadine. A starlet. A Natalie Wood type, which means that she looks a little like Natalie Wood but is much cheaper. She has freckles but is otherwise conventionally beautiful. They can cover the freckles with makeup or, if the movie wants it or allows it, they can leave them to declare her innocence and next-doorishness. Chestnut hair, but that too can be adjusted.

That's enough description, really. All the girls out there look much alike and are slender and pretty. Most of them are beautiful, which is a burdensome advantage. The worst part isn't the reiterative humiliation but the occasional moments of hope that come from getting a tiny part in a movie (a dancer in a crowd on a nightclub floor maybe or, even better, a hatcheck girl with a line to deliver). These occur just often enough so that a girl may decide to stick it out a little longer. What's to lose? (Or what more is there to lose?)

Nadine wasn't stupid, which was also a mixed blessing. She wasn't an intellectual, surely, but she had a quick mind, could be amused by a joke, and was able to speak in sentences with subordinate clauses in them. She also had a gift for sizing people up (not that it did her much good at that point).

They met, Abner told me, at one of those parties in Santa Monica that was a celebration of some wisp of good fortune—a young woman had been cast as one of the dancers in a musical number that was an homage (or parody or rip-off) of a Busby Berkley extravaganza with twenty white pianos and lots of girls in bizarre costumes descending curved staircases. It was two weeks' work that paid what she thought of as real money. And she invited everyone she knew and anyone they knew for white wine and fondue, which was then supposed to be fun but was unarguably cheap. Abner turned up as a friend of a friend and after a while found himself talking to Nadine, or, more specifically, listening as she complained about how disappointed she was in the life she and her friends were leading.

It is not difficult to imagine. She had one of those long dancer's bodies. I think she had been a dancer once but had done something to one of the bones of a foot and had been advised to give it up. So she was an actress. Her large well-set eyes always looked a little regretful, even when she was smiling. She was almost certainly a friend of the celebrating hostess. She wore, I'd like to think, a rather shapeless sweater knitted on very large needles, so as not to show herself off too much. (That was for business.) They were talking. Abner was looking very sporty in a blue and white striped *marinière*, white duck pants, and a blue kerchief around his neck. Very San Tropez. The fact that his hairline was already receding gave him an air of distinction.

"They're supposed to be dream factories," she says, "but what they turn out is mostly nightmares. Way beyond anything Nathaniel West ever imagined. A friend of mine was at a casting call and was asked to stay for what she thought was an interview. It was an interview, but not for the part. This producer said to Betsy—that's her name-- 'You're a pretty girl, so here's the deal. An apartment, a credit card, a car, and a thousand a week. Take it or leave it.' 'For what?' she asked. 'What the fuck do you think?'"

"Well, it was crude, maybe, but at least straightforward," Abner says. "He wasn't misleading her or letting her think it was something more romantic. It was honest." And gives her a look in which he lowers his face but raises his eyes, as if to ask what she or Betsy could have expected.

"It's not funny," she says.

"Yes, it is," he says. "It's so surprisingly candid. But what happened? Did she take the deal?"

Now Nadine laughs. "What do you think? If you'd been in her place, what would you do?"

"Don't know," Abner says. "It's nasty but tempting. I wouldn't blame her either way."

"She turned him down. She thought it was the last straw. Or a sign. She went back to Chicago."

I think it was the unvarnished truth of what goes on around here, but probably everywhere else, too. It's a meat market, plain and simple," Abner says.

"Some men are just awful."

"And some women, too. It sounds to me as though he's made that proposition before. Sometimes with better results. The worst you can say about it is that it's very businesslike."

She laughs and Abner goes to fetch her another glass of wine. She has impressed him as much by her mention of Nathaniel West as by her looks.

When he returns, she asks him what he does. He shakes his head and admits that he's a writer. "I hoped so," she says and gives him her phone number. "It would be good to talk again. Nobody out here has made me laugh in forever."

A big deal? Certainly not, but it is the beginning of a friendship, which is as much a rarity out there as laughter.

Of course there is also the joke about the Polish starlet who is so dumb that she fucks the writer, but we won't go there. Abner would have thought of it but my guess is that he wouldn't have told her.

We return for a moment to the touchy question of Abner's sexual... preferences? Proclivities? Inclinations? All the words are charged now and political, but back then they were unspoken. I must explain how innocent we were. One of my college roommates turned out to be a prominent gay poet, and I had no idea at the time that he was either gay or a poet. I wasn't alone in my obtuseness. At some recent reunion or other, there was a panel discussion about gay life at Yale in the fifties, and many of my classmates—then in their late fifties—had no idea that there had been any gays at all. (These weren't stupid people; I suppose they just couldn't see what they weren't looking for.)

What bothers me now is that we were good friends and there was a significant part of his life I never knew about. There were a couple of others in my prep school class whom I later discovered to be gay, and I felt a similar sadness for them, that they were required to pose as straight. Any kind of imposture is likely to be stressful, making you feel separated and lonely. It wasn't a secret that any of them felt safe in confiding. Yale's great poet was and still is Cole Porter of ambivalent (just barely) sexuality. My ambition was to acquire some of the gays' brio without the physical part of it--only because that wasn't in the repertoire of my appetites. I don't care for smoked oysters either, but I don't think of that as a character flaw.

Abner must have been bi. He once referred to his illegitimate daughter whose mother was a member of the royal family of Portugal—the kind of thing that was too implausible for anybody to make up. (Unless that was the point and the reason for his having made it up.) Anyway the point of all this is that Nadine would probably have sensed his indeterminacy--young women are better able to do this than their male counterparts. Did she find it comforting—that he wouldn't be all over her? Or tempting? Some girls think of gays as a challenge, the way French women used to think about priests (back when they thought about priests). But it could have been much simpler. It could just as easily have been the neckerchief and the facial expression (he always looked alert as if he were concentrating on whatever one was saying), or the traces he still had of that lazy Texas accent, which made his wit all the more surprising.

But it is hopeless to try to find reasons for the way they clicked. There are important conjunctions in our lives and we know little about them. Novels, poems, and plays mostly project what happens afterward, but the *coup de foudre* itself remains a mystery, beyond our understanding and control. Cupid's darts come suddenly and from out of the blue, or at least from somewhere else. Which is what makes these moments wonderful.

They became friends and then good friends. For her, it was comforting to have a smart young man (only two years older than she was) sharing her small triumphs and large disappointments. She got a part in a movie, but oddly enough her looks had little to do with it. This time, she was in the chorus of *Zombies Love Mambo*, and in her costume and makeup scarcely recognizable as human let alone pretty. She told him about a screen test for a part where she could appear as a person with, as she put it, "her face hanging out." They had a nice dinner together in an amiably phony Italian place with plastic vine leaves in swags around the brick walls and chianti fiascos in straw baskets in arched niches, and he made her laugh and cheered her up.

And for him? She was good company and, while I'm only guessing, could have been a plausible subject for a short story, a novel, a screenplay, or all of the above. She had an edge. Think *Butterfield 8* or *Breakfast at Tiffany's*. The plot doesn't matter so much as the appealing combination of fragility and courage that those women display and that he saw in Nadine. I don't suppose he took notes. (I'm not sure he ever took notes at Yale, for that matter.) But he acclimated himself to her behavior and habits of speech as he contemplated her being. These are not bad habits. People don't have to be writers do this, because love and fascination are parts of each other. (I suppose it could follow that for non-writers, the experience of paying this kind of attention is even more astonishing because they haven't spent much of their lives training themselves to do it.)

Did they go to bed together? They must have. In fact, I can't imagine not. Whatever his preference, Abner was certainly capable of having sex with women other than members of the house of Braganza, and Nadine was gorgeous. She'd have been put off if they hadn't. It wouldn't necessarily have ended the friendship but would have changed it. I knew a woman who said she loved having queers around: they were amusing and you could send them out for cigarettes and Tampax. (No, I don't quite know what that means, except that it was fondly dismissive.) But as I consider what happened afterwards, I believe each of them had to have been at least a plausible partner, if that makes any sense.

Assuming that there was sex, it would have been only occasional and on her terms. She could suppose he was simply unwilling to seem importunate. That would have been, in LA, something of a novelty. Most girls in the business come to think of hundreds and hundreds of erect penises all pointing at them like compass needles all day and most of the night. With Abner, she could relax a little.

But even so, there would have been a new mode of communication. I am way out of my depth here and am just guessing, but even with more normal (normative?) couples, we are guessing. It is always a mystery, even to the participants. Mainly to the participants. Whatever they think they think, the body turns out to have its own opinions and this is one of the arenas in which it can express its views, saying to the self and the other the most unpredictable things. That is why there are all these novels out there, each of them an effort to understand what happens, and how, and with what consequences. And if you read enough of them, you don't learn much about love or sex, but only about novels, which was not at all the purpose of your inquiry.

Their couplings would have been at his place, probably. She shared a flat with a couple of other young hopefuls and, while they sometimes brought guys home to bed, she thought that was a bit icky. At his apartment, they had privacy. That would have been the first apartment, in Melrose maybe, which I never saw or heard about. It was at about this time that he moved to the converted boathouse in Malibu. A friend was going to Paris and needed a house- and cat-sitter. There was no mortgage. No sane banker would have lent money on a house that could be swept away by any medium-sized storm. But there were taxes, and if Abner could pay the taxes and take care of the cat, the friend would be appreciative. By then, Abner could afford to do that. He'd wised up a little and knew how much the Guild guys were getting for his kind of work. He never joined the guild but he raised his prices to a level just below theirs—so he was still a bargain.

The odd structure he lived in looked, at one end, the land side, like a bungalow. The other end had been kind of a barn door through which a boat could pass out to the launching dock. Now that the dock was gone, the barn door arrangement had been changed to a huge panel of plate glass that looked out at the ocean. Spectacular! I visited him there a couple of times, and it seemed like something glitzy from a Ross Hunter movie. In a movie, though, it wouldn't have been so noisy. On one side, there were big trucks barreling up and down the Pacific Coast Highway, and on the other there was the continual flushing of the Pacific Ocean. Sitting just a few feet apart, we had to yell to make ourselves understood. He said he didn't mind the truck noise. "You get used to it," he said, "the way people on Third Avenue got used to the El. Or said they did. Besides, weird things happen on that highway. There was a big furry thing that looked at first like a bear traveling north and it turned out to be Joanne Woodward's fur-covered Volkswagen. If it had been at night, it would have been less frightening. Bears don't have headlights." And then, with a quick grin, he added, "That's a title, isn't it?"

I rehearse that conversation because it is one of the few I can remember of many that made me feel as though we were on different, not quite parallel universes. Or to be less grandiose, I was again the country mouse listening wide-eared and wide-eyed to stories the city mouse was telling me. That some of them were hard to believe was only a guarantee of their authenticity: if Abner had been making them up, he'd have made them more plausible, if only out of craftsmanly pride.

✻

From time to time, we would exchange letters, continuing our old correspondence. I was living on Cape Cod at the time, and he was out there on the shore of the other ocean from which, occasionally, a thick envelope would arrive with his large scrawl on sheets of those yellow legal pads he liked. In this fitful way we managed to communicate something of the texture of our lives if not the details, even important ones. I have no idea, therefore, how and when the subject of marriage came up between them. It isn't at all difficult to make a reasonable guess. If I am right about Abner being bi, then it is improbable that he made the suggestion. Nadine then? She was living a stressful life and finding comfort and solace in Abner's company as well as pleasure in his bed. His boathouse was a cheerfully absurd and reassuring place to be. And above all, Abner was funny. No matter how angry or depressed Nadine might have been, he could make her laugh. And then he'd warn her about how, when she laughed, her nose would wrinkle—which would be a liability for a beauty queen. And she'd laugh at that, too.

So she suggests it. On one of those tranquil nights, maybe after smoking a little weed, she looks out at the moonlit Pacific and asks, "Do you think that maybe we should get married sometime?"

He laughs. She says it's not funny and seems hurt. Not deeply wounded but hurt. So he feels obliged to make nice.

"I wasn't laughing at the idea but … its abruptness. Sure, it'd be lovely for us to be married. But there are problems. Money, mostly. Neither of our careers is going well enough to be a reliable source of cash, as you must have noticed. And it isn't just the lack of it. What do we do when you hit it big and are suddenly rich beyond your wildest imaginings while I'm still scrabbling on the fringes, juggling credit card bills that, so far, I've been lucky enough to be able to pay off eventually. But it's not admirable. Or comfortable. And if we were married, I'd want you to admire me. We don't need to do another remake of *A Star is Born*, do we? The ocean Norman Maine walks into is right out there, isn't it?"

"You're exaggerating," she said.

"Life exaggerates."

"So you're turning me down?"

"No, not at all. Only for the moment. I'd love to marry you. But I'd hate for us to get divorced. That happens a lot out here."

She was quiet for a moment and then asked, "Where does that leave us, then?"

He kissed her forehead and asked, "Can we be engaged? People are generally happier when they're engaged than when they're married. Let's go with that for the time being."

"Sure," she said.

Was she satisfied with that? Was he? It is too late now to ask them, so all I can do is hazard guesses. As I do that, I realize that although we were friends, Abner and I really didn't know each other very well. (This is a chastening insight, but then how well do any of us know anyone else. Or even ourselves?) And I never met Nadine, which is a disadvantage. Still, sometimes less information is better, as in certain math problems. "No, no, don't tell me any more," Henry James used to say. When he had the nub of what he wanted—from someone's remark at a dinner table—he did not want to be distracted or constrained by extraneous details. Their engagement may not have been anything but a hope or perhaps a declaration of intention, but then Hollywood runs on intentions.

My hunch is that this would have been in some ways a familiar arrangement for him. She could have been like that picture of Mary on his dresser back at school, except that Nadine existed and was even present sometimes. Physically, but spiritually, too. The wispy filaments of those late-night conversations in bed turned out over the years to be their lifeline. Nothing else was real.

II

The last thing in the world I expected this to turn into was a scholarly essay on Henry James's attitude toward sex. Or, more precisely, sex and money, neither of which could be discussed back then in polite company. Maybe for James, the nastiness of the one cancelled out the naughtiness of the other. But beneath all the fuss and bother of the late novels, there is a barely restrained disgust about the British aristos marrying for money and the American heiresses marrying for titles and social prominence. It all looks perfectly respectable, but what he saw just below the surface was whoring and pimping, which may not in themselves have been shocking but did suggest a certain hypocrisy in the lofty attitudes of the Europeans. Americans have their faults, too, but we seldom try to pass them off as virtues.

What has this to do with anything? Abner, remember, had spent some time in France in the company of what was left of the aristocracy. Their basic assumptions were different from his--and ours. Over and over, a young girl in a Collette story becomes the mistress of a rich old man. The money is good and she learns from him to distinguish between the soup spoon and the bouillon spoon. Aside from everything else, it's an education for her. And when the old guy dies, she has money and can retire. She can, indeed, take a young lover and teach him about spoons. What impressed Abner, I should think, was how sensible an arrangement this was and how much more enlightening were the novels that explored this altitudinous terrain. I remember that we talked about this once or twice and were pleased that we shared a dislike of James and a fondness for Collette and, even more, Proust.

To marry for love is a relatively recent idea. It used to be that if two families had adjoining vineyards or fields, the sensible thing was to combine the two holdings to make a larger, more efficient property. One family has a son and the other a daughter. It's a merger more than a wedding, but there is nothing inherently wrong with that. What is love anyway but the mood of the moment, which, however powerful, is not a secure foundation for a future--as the divorce rate so clearly demonstrates. It is a romantic idea, coming from all those *romans*, which started out as propaganda for chastity. (And who, except for some crazy evangelicals, believes in that anymore?)

Nadine's career never quite took off. She was cast in a couple of B movies (there were B movies back then). She could deliver lines reasonably well, walk to her mark, and stop there without having to look down to see the chalk line on the floor. She told Abner that a lighting guy had told her she had really terrific ears, which was news to her. (Could she be an earring model?) She did land a couple of parts in major productions which paid well enough but these were so tiny, that they weren't vehicles in which she'd have been noticed. Even with those pretty ears. She got by but knew that as time passed the odds against her were greater with every passing month.

They still got together, Abner and Nadine, although sporadically. They would have dinner together or meet in bars. Or she'd come to spend the night with him. Their understanding was still in effect, that someday, when circumstances permitted, they might get married. In the meantime, they consoled each other with talk, reassurance, and *les tendresses bestiales.* Abner was now trying to write another novel. Or, rather, he was committed enough to the project to allude to it in his letters to me. I can't imagine that there weren't jottings that he'd made since *Is It Morning Already?* But none of them had turned into anything substantial enough for him to mention.

Ideally, a novelist has an idea, shrugs it off but then finds that it keeps returning, each time in a more complicated guise and always more insistently; only then, figuring that it might have some special significance for him, does he sit down and begin to scribble notes, perhaps even making a list of characters and a rough outline. Writers' lives are seldom ideal, and my guess is that, out there in the insubstantiality of the movie world and the flimsiness of that converted boathouse, he needed a project. And he may have been trying (too hard?) to do a book in order to reassert his idea of himself, not as somebody who had once published a novel, but as a novelist. First person and present tense. There were lots of writers--Faulkner, Fitzgerald, and Isherwood, among others—who put in time out there but never let it define them. It can be done but is an act of will and needs both craftsmanship and equipoise. And maybe *sangfroid.* Nadine, meanwhile, was getting by but was increasingly discouraged about her prospects. One night she reminded Abner of her friend, Betsy and the deal that crude producer had offered. "I don't know now what I'd have done. Or would do now. Go home, the way she did? Or take it."

"Would you? Really?"

"I can't say for sure, but what Betsy did seems cowardly. As an actress, you come to think of your body as an instrument, something you work with that isn't quite yourself. You kiss a guy because it's in the script. You take off your shirt and flash your tits because the producer wants to excite the little boys in the audience. It's not your body after a while, but a body that happens to belong to you. And that you rent out. Is that crazy?"

"Not out here," Abner said. Then he asked, "Why? Have you had an offer like that?"

"Not exactly that. But offers. All the time. And I ask myself each time if it's worth it. They say that Grace Kelly would fuck a headwaiter for a good table. Do I admire that? Or what?"

"Or putting it another way, was she a whore or a grownup?"

"Aren't they the same thing?" she asked.

"Maybe so."

He wanted, of course, to ask. Had she accepted any? But thought better of it. If she wanted to tell him, she would. Wasn't that why she had brought up the subject in the first place? Perhaps she intended to tell him something but had changed her mind and backed off. It didn't matter that much. If not now, it would be later. He had the odd idea that she was testing him, waiting for him to ask, and might even be pleased that he wasn't. With each passing moment of silence, he felt closer to her and imagined her feeling the same way.

It is a paradox of love that it while it often manifests itself in jealousy, it can also work in an opposite way, in the toleration of whatever the beloved may do or may have done. The latter is probably closer to that impossible ideal, which recognizes the otherness of the other and not only accepts but celebrates it. Who of us is confident enough in himself—and in her—to go beyond possessiveness that way? "Teach us the difference between hunger and love," Auden says somewhere; it is a difficult challenge. Oddly, if my guesses are correct, Abner's bisexuality helped him achieve this loftiness. Or it might have been *tout court* a demonstration of his generosity of spirit.

What would we expect of such a character? It's not an irrelevance because he was a writer, or at least thought of himself as one. And some writers consider what the character they are playing in life would do. Or to put it another way, what would a grownup do? The fact that Grace Kelly would fuck a headwaiter for the good table is at first interesting because it is shocking. But it is also suggestive of a certain courage on her part, a willingness to use whatever she had when it was important enough to do so. That's Hollywood after all. But the real grownup in her case was Prince Rainier, who must have known about her behavior but didn't care. What had it to do with him? Princess Grace would be altogether different from the actress, except perhaps in terms of her looks, which were terrific. I'm maundering here, I admit, but maundering is as likely a path to the truth as any other.

Let's say then that they were friends, lovers, loving friends… They could trust each other, as many loving pairs cannot. They may have assumed certain things, but none of it mattered. It was in many ways an enviable state. And it was the necessary precondition for the conversation that is not, after all, so surprising. Nadine asked him one night whether she would mind if she got married.

"You're kidding, aren't you?"

"No, I'm serious. I have a scheme."

"I love schemes," he said, "at least in theory. What's this one? Or shouldn't I ask?"

She told him what she had in mind, which was at the same time ridiculous and classic. Very French. Collette would have approved but Henry James would have been troubled by it. The risks, in literature at any rate, are considerable but almost always interesting. In real life it must happen that a plan like hers works sometimes. Not all love affairs end badly, even though that is what novelists report. But by its nature, the evidence of fiction is, if you'll excuse the term, anecdotal. What Nadine proposed was that she marry Jason (Jay)Bishop (*né* Bishkopf) a seventy-eight-year-old producer in parlous health; then, in a few years, she would inherit his wealth, or at least the spousal minimum (half, I think, under California law). She and Abner could then marry and live comfortably for the rest of their lives.

"What's wrong with his health?" Abner asked.

"He's had several heart attacks. He has to be careful about everything he does."

Abner nodded as he digested this information. "So your plan is to fuck him to death?"

"Essentially. That's what will make it tolerable. Or even fun."

"You're a wicked girl," he said.

"Isn't that one of the things you like about me most?"

"Love about you."

"Good. Love about me."

"And can this really happen? Has he proposed?"

"He will."

"And you'll accept?"

"Probably," she said. "That's what we're talking about, isn't it?"

"And if I said no?"

"I don't know. I might not do it," she said. "But why would you say no?"

"Just asking."

"It's unknown territory," she said. "In a way, that also makes it interesting, doesn't it?"

❊

We do not really discuss questions of such import. Rather, there is a process of digestion, a long murky brood from which a decision eventually emerges. For Abner, the terms were reasonably clear: He was sufficiently clear-eyed to see that if he tried to hold on to Nadine, he would probably lose her, and that was the last thing he wanted to do. His adventure with the Portuguese *infanta*—if there really was one—would have been clearly defined from the beginning as a brief encounter with no possible future. Still, assuming that Nadine acted on her plan, there would be a sadness that accompanied the celebration of her success. Would he be jealous? He loved Nadine in his way, and she, in hers, loved him. So what was the best thing he could do for her? This marriage, however calculating and unsavory, would get her out of an environment that was even more unappealing. And he could not take a producer of horror movies seriously. Jay had produced that zombie movie in which Nadine had appeared a few years before, and now they'd bumped into each other in London where she had been shooting a commercial.

Abner was certainly in no position to offer her the refuge that Jay could and, as far as he could see, never would be. The confidence he'd had when *Is It Morning Already?* came out was so far gone that he could hardly remember it. If there were to be a sequel to it, the title would possibly have been *False Dawn*. He had been after all just another ambitious kid with dreams that never came to anything. (He was more than that, of course: I'm talking about his state of mind, as far as I dare imagine it.)

Could the plan actually work? He doubted it, but there was nothing specific he could think of that would make it impossible. Whatever Nadine thought, their understanding offered her a glimmer of hope. It may have been a mere fancy, but it softened the judgment she might otherwise make of her own behavior. Marriage to Jay would be a way to extricate herself from the seamy world of auditions and screen tests in which every passing day was a blow. She was only twenty-seven and looked wonderful, but there were seventeen-year-olds showing up with her at casting calls and they had a longer shelf life.

Is this right? More or less, this is the way the conversation was likely to have gone, both the spoken and unspoken parts of it. But the tone would have been different, wittier and battier. Abner had that odd ability to lighten a mood with some unexpected flash. For instance he once said, "The advantage flowers have over us is that they have their sexual organs on their heads so that there's less confusion. They know what they are about. We have to figure it out all the time and we keep getting it wrong."

It was about this time, I suppose, that the letter from Abner reached me with a surprising couple of paragraphs well down in the several pages of text. (He wrote with a broad-nibbed pen in large cursive letters and the result was a letter that could have been a couple of pages of typescript but took twelve or so of these sheets that were folded up and stuffed into a manila envelope on which there would invariably be more stamps than were required, as if having a postage scale within reach was somehow parsimonious and tacky.) He was rambling on about one thing and another, Hollywood gossip and odd remarks he'd heard, and then there was a surprising divagation about the later novels of Henry James: "What was old Hen getting at with those square dances about sex and money? Was he just screwing around with the complexity of it? Or did he have something actually to say about how Merton and Kate could perfectly well have been happy if only they hadn't been so stupid? Marrying Milly for her money is a reasonable idea when Lord Mark talks about it, but you have to be a grownup—or a European--if you expect it to work. (Americans are always the dangerous innocents in Henry James' fiction: write for an hour.)"

Something along those lines. I think he may have suggested that he was thinking about a novel that might address these questions. Or just clarify old Hen's ambiguous answer. But I can't avoid now drawing the obvious conclusion—that he was doing both, thinking about himself and Nadine and Jay Bishop and their situation, of which at that time I was ignorant, and distancing it by talking about *The Wings of the Dove*. He'd never been much interested in James, so I took the surprising inquiry as having to do with something else. I supposed he was talking about a treatment he'd been assigned. Or a novel he might write, while he was in fact asking for practical answers or even advice. He'd been so delicately oblique that it never crossed my mind that he might be talking about his own life.

Should I feel guilty for having been obtuse and not having replied in a more helpful way? I don't think so. Advice wasn't what he wanted or needed. People seldom take advice anyway, even from friends. Especially from friends. And I didn't and don't have the wisdom to tell anyone what to do. My hope is that he was just ventilating, enjoying the writing of that piece of the letter the way he enjoyed any other paragraph with that lovely feeling of the pen in the fingers as it formed letters, words, and shapely sentences. Maybe he just liked to woolgather on paper with a sympathetic reader in mind.

It happened. With or without Abner's approval, Nadine married old Jaybird. Old, old Jay. Almost fifty years her senior. I remember a discussion I had in France once with an acute observer of that nation's folkways who told me that schoolmates, even when they were old and distinguished, continued to *tutoyer* each other. He suggested that when there were just a couple of people left from General de Gaulle's *école* class, they would still address him as "tu," while everyone else in the world would say "vous." "Except maybe Madame de Gaulle?" I countered. And he replied with a wry smile,

"I wouldn't bet on it."

We don't have such refined gradations in American social intercourse, but if they had been French, I can imagine Nadine finding elaborate periphrases to avoid using "tu" to him. Never mind father, he was old enough to be her grandfather. It is quite reasonable for young girls to marry rich elderly men. Because of their age, they are not excessively demanding about sex. Nadine was certainly old enough to know what she was doing. And in Hollywood, there isn't much that shocks, anyway. I was not aware of these nuptials. I can't remember that Abner had mentioned Nadine to me more than a couple of times. And if he had? And if I had come across some mention of the weddings in newspapers? I still wouldn't have given it much thought.

I would never have supposed that Abner and Nadine had their odd, novelistic arrangement. They could meet, although not too often and always in public places. Nadine could never be sure that Jay wasn't having her followed so that he'd have grounds for divorce if he ever decided to do that. They were therefore careful and would have coffee and maybe a piece of pastry from time to time. Her story to Jay, if she ever needed one, would be that Abner was one of her gay friends from the old days and was amusing. This was half true. What she liked and soon came to rely on was Abner's understanding, his intuitive grasp of her self-consciousness about the bargain she had made. He never expressed disapproval. They no longer spoke of their plan, but each could assume that it was still in effect—that when Jay died sooner or later she would inherit and they would then marry. This thought enabled her to consider herself as something other than Jay's sex slave. (Indentured servant, maybe?) But Abner wasn't jealous, sexually and I wonder if that may have been the gay culture, which was, and I expect still is, permissive about such matters. Abner did think it wasn't at all funny that Jay's housekeeper was a practical nurse, so that, on those occasions when he felt like "fooling around" (do people still say that?) there would be medical help immediately available with a supply of nitroglycerin and a defibrillator. Fucking him to death, therefore, wasn't going to be so easy. Nadine told Abner that under these circumstances she never initiated sex. And even when he did, there was the element of danger. "It isn't love," she confided, "but it's something. Anger? Defiance? A combat of some kind." She made an airy gesture with her hand. "But a connection."

"I see," he said, with a sly grin. "At least it isn't boring."

"You're a love," she said with an intimate moue as she touched the back of his hand, which was the limit of the public intimacy they could dare.

Abner's news for her was that he had a job, not just one of these month-long quickies but one that would extend for a year or more. Nothing wonderful, but not too demeaning, either. He had been asked to ghostwrite the autobiography of Helmut Felsenfeld, a director who had fled the Nazis years ago but whose English still wasn't very good. "There are a lot of guys like that. MOS for instance means 'mitout sound' in screenplays because that's what those German immigrants from UFA used to say and even write in scripts and it's traditional now. But they didn't need language if they could frame a shot well and knew how to light a scene. He hasn't worked much lately but he's got a certain reputation. We meet once a week or so at his place and he talks into a tape recorder while I ask questions. And I bring him last week's pages. There's lunch, usually a salad. And he's got this cat gymnasium in the living room but no cats."

She cocked her head to one side and raised her eyebrows in skepticism or dubiety.

"It's for cats of his who are dead but whose ghosts, he is sure, come back to play on it at night. That's typical," he said. "There's a good bit of craziness, but I'm managing. I can hold on."

He didn't have to tell her until when or refer to their plan; her acknowledgement with a slight nod was eloquent enough.

Aside from my connection with Abner, I'm interested in these events because there are few examples of that kind of love, reliable but not possessive. In *The Wings of the Dove*, about which Abner had asked, Milly Theale displays that exemplary, generous love, both for Densher and for her friend Kate Kroy. But we must remember that Milly is dying (so she can afford to be less grasping than most of us would be) and that she is likened to an angel—or is it the Holy Spirit? —with all that "dove" business. Old Hen is therefore telling us that this is an extreme case, which is probably why it interested him.

I said earlier that Abner and I didn't much care for James, and when we were undergraduates, we didn't. He wrote long, dense books, and they are not fun to race through when they've been assigned. Beyond that, while you're reading you are also looking for something to say in a five-page paper. These books are not cadavers, even if English teachers treat them that way. They are, if they are any good at all, living creatures, genies we can summon up by running our eyes along the lines of text. No one under thirty should read late Henry James. In connection with this story about Abner and Nadine, I went back and reread the novel. It was much better than I remembered. But inasmuch as it hadn't changed, the improvement must have been in me.

Here, instead of Milly, who was more or less a volunteer, the dying person was supposed to be Jay, but he was unaware of the plot. (Probably he had never read any Henry James.) In any case, he wasn't dying. He had heart trouble, but so do a lot of people. And they are maintained for a long time by the miracle (or curse) of modern medicine. He was old, sure, but not that old. I'm now the age he was at the time of these events, and I'm a little arthritic but generally feel fine. On the other hand, when I was in my early thirties, I thought of 78 as positively geriatric. In any event, while the plan Nadine had dreamed up wasn't altogether implausible, it required a great deal of patience and a lot of luck, and still it wasn't at all certain to succeed.

Months go by. Two or two and a half years, in fact. The arrangement for Abner to be the ghostwriter for the not-quite-has-been director falls apart. Felsenfeld has been showing the manuscript around, ostensibly for criticism and advice, but really as a way to attract some attention to his name, remind the world of who he was, and let them know that he's still around. And available. It was less a book than it was a résumé he could circulate gracefully. Felsenfeld gets hired as a "lighting consultant." So Abner is let go with an expansive *danke shön* and a modest present (a tip, really: less than two week's pay). He's out of work. After several weeks of unemployment he gets a job writing a script for a television pilot, for which he has to join the Writers' Guild. But it's still money. Then he hears from his sister, Frannie, back in Lubbock who tells him that their mother has had a stroke and that he should come home right away. One can't refuse a demand like that, so he goes. And stays. Not that he can do anything useful, but Lurlene is convinced that without someone there to look after things the caretakers, visiting nurses, and therapists will steal her ear rings.

"Her ear rings?"

"You know what I mean. Ear rings. Anything." (Frannie reports this with exasperation. Lurlene is their mother, but even so, there is a limit, Frannie thinks, to what children can be expected to put up with.) Frannie has a job as a paralegal and can't be around the house all the time. But Abner can. Why not? He's a writer and can write here as well as anywhere else, can't he? (No, but try to explain this to a determined woman who, even before the stroke, wasn't easy to talk to.) There's nothing to keep him in Hollywood, is there? (It's Malibu, but Abner has given up on explaining the distinction.)

He tells Frannie and his mother about his job writing the director's autobiography, not bothering to mention that it has ended, but they are not impressed. After all, he's doing it for the money, isn't he? Is that what he wanted to spend his time and talent doing? And in any case, which is more important, this nobody-ever-heard-of-him director or Abner's own mother? He won't have to *do* anything. The caretaker helps her go to the toilet and take showers.

What is particularly difficult about this is that he can't even begin to explain to Frannie about Nadine. Whom he doesn't see very often and who is anyway married to Bishop. She'd laugh at him. (And would probably be right.) So he's beaten without even going through the motions of a fight, and he knows it. He agrees. He flies back to LA to pack up his books and clothes and ship them home, and find another cat-sitter from his friend. Then, he comes back to Lubbock—without even having seen Nadine. It's a catastrophe.

One of those thick letters arrives in my mailbox in which he announces his return to Lubbock and attributes it to "farce majeure. " It was a handwritten letter, like all the others, and I almost missed his little joke, but there it was, with that *a* where the *o* should be. He included an ad for a big truck rally from the *Avalanche Journal* on which he'd written in grease pencil "FUN???" The *Avalanche Journal?* Jesus!

There is one advantage in the distance between Lubbock and LA, which is roughly a thousand miles. If he had been living in Malibu while she was in Newport Beach, the proximity would have been tantalizing and burdensome. Even though it would have been ruinous, he could at least have imagined jumping into a car, tooling south, picking her up, and taking her off into the hills somewhere. The distance between them was an insulation through which unexpected, painful sparks could not fly. There were fantasies, his and hers, probably, but they were more free and dreamlike. Abner was well enough aware that his vision of her was less and less actual, but when we are in love, we tend to dress the real person in the designs of our desires. The wraiths they have become approach ever closer to the perfection of whatever we fancy. A real person requires accommodation and adjustments, as the mental simulacrum never does.

He wondered what she was doing? How was she living? Did she and Jay get on well together? (And which answer would he have found more uncomfortable?) Each of them became a presence in the other's fantasies. For Nadine, he must have been the source of a reliable love that was an attractive alternative to her life in Newport Beach, as constant as the eternal light in a synagogue. He was her cicisbeo, her faithful *cavalier servente*, whose function was to be the window that let light into her the world's oubliette. Even if she didn't avail herself of it, he represented the possibility of an eventual escape, the thought of which helped her breathe. She could take it for granted that off in Lubbock he was thinking about her and whenever she thought of him, she could suppose that the instant might well be reciprocal. She was usually alone at these moments, brushing her teeth, for instance, when he would appear in her mind, as if he were observing her and smiling sympathetically, and maybe making some wry observation—that life is what happens when you're not flossing.

Nonsense? Of course it is, but we lead more of our lives in the land of nonsense than we are willing to admit. It is a comfortable refuge. Who hasn't had conversations of this kind with the dead? Or long-lost loves? She was a not-quite-fanciful figure who might present herself at any moment as an alternative to Lubbock. She could call. The phone could ring any time with her announcement that Jay had at last booted the barrel and her command that he come out there. Sometimes he toyed with the idea that that she could come to Lubbock, which was incongruous enough to be comical.

Lurlene recovered a little but was not yet herself. And never would be. She walked now with one of those four-footed canes and her left foot dragged a little. The left side of her face didn't move, which made her expressions odd and slightly menacing. She grew used to having Abner around and was reluctant to let him leave. For his part, it was impossible to argue—you can't stay here and take care of your mother? What kind of self-absorbed monster have you become? After all we've done for you, Bitsy? You can write here perfectly well. We have electric lights and mailboxes here in Lubbock. We have stores that sell ink. What else do you need? If you were serious about it, this would be a fine place for you to work. But you don't really write anymore, do you? You did one funny novel and now that you don't have to prove anything, you can't get yourself together to do it again. That's how you've always been, brilliant but lazy. Your father said we were spoiling you and he was right. And on and on.

The ironic thing was that here in Lubbock, where there were few distractions, he could think almost uninterruptedly about Nadine—and was even driven to do so. He could hide from his mother, as he had to do, in daydreams about Nadine and in reading--Joseph Conrad for a while and then Walter Scott, and a few modern novels, like *Death of the Fox*, which he just loved. And to keep from going utterly mad, he could even write.

About? He never said. It could have been that he was just pretending to write, to himself, first of all, but also to his mother, Nadine, and maybe even to me. To maintain the fiction. (Is there such a thing as fictional fiction?) Do you have to put an actual pen to real paper in the long haul of the longhand? The chances are that he did write, not inconceivably about some version of his own predicament, which is what smart writers often do. Write about what you know, they say, as if Shakespeare used to hang out with kings and vacation on the seacoast of Bohemia. But in some disguised way, a mood or a kind of pain or a dream can inform anything. And for his sake, I prefer to imagine that he was writing—or trying to—about absence. There isn't much fiction about that painful predicament. (Chekhov's "Lady with the Dog," perhaps?)

It isn't static. Over time, its quality changes, becoming deeper or more bitter. The situation remains the same, but the thought that she was thinking of him becomes ever so slightly diminished in clarity and persuasiveness from week to week. We could compare it to the grief for a death. The parent or lover or child is no less dead, but the grief become less unbearable, even deserting its post for minutes and then hours at a time. It also universalizes, because other people, too, have gone through it. One's apartness turns out not to be so special. And one resents it for its infidelity.

And yet, on the other hand, if this is the human condition, it is surely worth writing about in some way. He might have played with the notion of time, which is one of the strategies of fiction that makes it different from the lives we lead in the domain of fact. We are always in the present. Characters in novels can remember and anticipate, of course, but more than that, they can actually go back, take up whatever gossamer existence they have in memory or decamp and set up housekeeping in the future, that habitat of fear and desire. Too intellectual and abstract for Abner? He might not have framed his thoughts in such words but, surely, he'd have been capable of considering them.

He might even have tried to figure out--as I have done, too--some odd arrangement in which parallel universes allow for very different variations on the thoughts and actions of a given moment. She is cruising along the Pacific Coast Highway in a tomato-soup red convertible with wisps of her hair that have escaped from her kerchief streaming behind her. Or, no she is in her bedroom, doing crossword puzzles and watching the clock waiting for it to be late enough for her to assume that Jay has fallen asleep. Better yet, have her in some sidewalk café they used to go to together, lingering over a cappuccino.

We don't get any of this in *The Wings of the Dove*, not because James wasn't aware of these oddities but rather because he wasn't comfortable with humor. His trouble, as a writer and, I'd be willing to bet, as a person was his inability to laugh. Or trust in the truth of what's funny. Milly is attractive enough, but she is too damned serious, so that she is never aware of the comedy of her situation.

✳

The further complication--or call it a refinement--was that he and Nadine weren't merely the prisoners of time and space. They were also Jay's prisoners. He was the one who, just by continuing to breathe and have a heartbeat, was keeping them apart. He didn't know this... Or maybe he did after a while. Why not? He was a movie guy, a story merchant, and with a lot of free time on his hands, he might well have wondered about Nadine's frame of mind. She hadn't married him for love. He knew that and didn't mind it. Enjoyed it, even. But the ordinary explanation would have been that she was just lazy and found this an easier life than working. Or, complicate it a little and figure that she was an actress. It could well be that this was just another role she had been offered and she was willing to play it because it was better than going to casting calls and doing screen tests. The sex? It was relatively infrequent, and not too burdensome. What he really wanted from her was entertaining company. And to show off a beautiful young girl on his arm at dinner parties for the other geezers to admire and envy. What she got out of that part of it was an impressive wardrobe. All women, and especially all actresses, like to play dress-up.

Is it also no great a stretch of the imagination to suppose that at some moment of irritation or anger or rebelliousness, such as there are in all marriages, Nadine hurled the information about Abner and their arrangement at him as if it were a weapon, making it clear that they were just waiting for him to die so they could marry. And if that had happened, would he have been furious? Or amused? Delighted even? Probably not surprised. He could he have expected that this was the case and might have taken some satisfaction to hear her confirm what he had always supposed. The most an old man can hope for with a much younger wife is fondness, a pastel simulacrum of love that has its charms. Passion is unlikely, but this protracted imposture might have been enough to create a constant seething somewhere in her soul. The more she cared about Abner, the greater her discomfort while she had to display good manners to him, which is the least a husband ought to expect. If he was right in these vague surmises, then her performance would be more difficult--and more praiseworthy--that he had first realized. He wasn't any kind of intellectual but he was surely crafty and had been in the business long enough to know that it doesn't make much difference what an actor is thinking, just as long as he or she has the look the role requires and moves in an interesting way. You care what Lassie is thinking? Or Flipper? Or Gregory Peck, whose range wasn't a whole hell of a lot greater than the first two? (Actually there were four or five Lassies, who shared the character's tricks.) Appearances are the only reality there is. The industry teaches people hard lessons and Bishop had learned them well. As Horatio says at the end of *Hamlet*, "The rest is horseshit."

In his last years, he was only tangentially in the movie business. He had produced pictures and had made money doing it, but there was less risk and a lot less work in just having lunch, which meant arranging financing for other people's projects. All those cards you see in the main titles that mean nothing to the audience—A Sisyphus Picture; An Intergalactic Production in association with Gatkes Enterprises and Anaphora Unlimited; Presented by Memorable Films—refer to people or outfits that do what Jay was doing, making bets or covering someone else's. The production of the actual movie might almost be an afterthought. (Often it is.) Certainly, the contracts are more interesting than most of the scripts, but then the lawyers enjoy the advantage of knowing who their audience is.

Abner looked Bishop up and found out what he could about him, not because he was genuinely interested but only to reduce him from spectral generality to a smaller, tamer specificity. It was a relief to discover that, aside from the money, there was nothing impressive about him. Abner didn't have to worry about any possible confusion on Nadine's part that might promote Bishop from an instrument in their plan to some kind of actual humanity, never mind "artist".

The reverse of that, which Abner realized was just as likely, was that all three had reduced themselves to cogs in a complicated piece of engineering, one of those clocks, say, that has its works on display so that you watch as wheels turn and gears move and don't even care what time it is as you gaze in fascination at the intricate machinery.

Or all four, because it was possible to include Lurlene, whose not absolutely unreasonable demands were keeping him in Lubbock. He had never had much connection to the place when he'd been a kid. Now, it was a weird theme park in which the rides were all about his childhood. The townspeople looked to have been hired to dress up and walk around feigning chores and appointments, but all according to a script that issued from some Disney-like office far away. It was unreal but at the same time tacky, an elaborate but pointless manipulation of matter, space, and time. If you can't trust those, what can you rely on?

There is a real Lubbock, of course, with actual people in it, but these do not preclude the notional Lubbock Abner lived in and shared with me. His letters were full of fantasies about the place, and just as Gore Vidal ignored the facts on the ground in *Duluth*, so did Abner and I invent whatever we liked, turning Lubbock Christian University into the more candid and accurate Lubbock Evangelical Snake-Handling Pentecostal School of Cosmetology, in which a row of life-sized crucified figures—think of the scene in "Spartacus"--took the place of the great allée of elm trees at Penn State. Lubbock is named after Thomas Lubbock, a Texas Ranger (no kidding!) but we preferred to imagine him as a faro dealer who was the only survivor of the Monterey shoot-out of 1887. (Old Lubbock and Monterey were separate towns that combined in 1890 to form the modern city.) Sometimes, he would write to tell me stuff that could pass as nonsense but turned out to be true. Who would suppose, for instance that the Texas Tech Dairy Barn is listed in the National Register of Historic Places? It is. You can look it up. None of this was particularly witty, I'm afraid, but I mention it as a demonstration of Abner's claustrophobic feeling that made him yearn for an escape to a place where he could breathe--even Cloudcuckooland. What, after all, could be more nonsensical than the real Lubbock or the real Duluth? There must be bars in Lubbock, but probably not gay bars. And the others? Sports bars, I'd think, with good old boys in boots and Stetsons whooping it up and doing line dancing on Friday nights. These were not Abner's natural compañeros.

Mapmakers put fictional towns on their maps so they can assert copyright should anyone try to pirate their work. If somebody else's map has a Franklin's Bend, say, off in the woods of Montana, they can demonstrate that they've been ripped off, because there isn't any such place. Lubbock does exist, but just barely. I've never been there or, aside from Abner, known anyone who has.

Or wait a minute. I do remember a friend of mine telling me about a reading he did at Texas Tech. The campus is dry. It is even forbidden to use empty liquor bottles for decorative purposes. My friend, George, had heard about this and was prepared. No booze before the reading or at dinner. So he had a pint of Scotch in his suitcase for personal use after his show-and-tell was finished. He did what he was supposed to do, read poems, talked with the students about the writing life, made chit-chat with faculty members at the small dinner party in his honor, and then, finally, went back to his room to open the Chivas. He was a guy who likes to read in bed. And have a sip now and then. By the time he had turned off the light, the bottle was empty. Now, who in the world puts an empty bottle into his luggage? He put it in the wastebasket in the morning, packed up, and left. And two days later he got a phone call from the assistant professor of English, one of his former students, who had invited him. The entire campus was buzzing with the news that the guest had left a whiskey bottle in his wastebasket. The department was scandalized and, naturally, they all blamed him. George, too, but he was gone. So the assistant professor, who was still there, was getting heat. He was reporting all this to George because it was funny. "Tell them you talked to me about it and I said I was sorry and didn't know the rules," George said. Or tell them I told them to go and fuck themselves. Whichever you prefer."

So that's Lubbock.

❖

What happens to secrets in fiction is all but irrelevant to what goes on in the real world. Mum is the word (from Henry VI, I think). But also from the way it involves pressing the lips together on the first *m*, opening them, and closing them on the second, which is not merely onomatopoetic but a dramatization. (Is this etymologically correct? Who knows? Who cares?)

The curious relationship between Nadine and Jay must have evolved, either into a constant, low-level enmity or else to a mutual toleration that could sometimes be amusing enough to approach friendship. Either way, one or another would have figured (or blurted) it out. Spilled the beans. A while back, I supposed that she might have wanted to hurt him, to demonstrate her independence or her indifference to him, or to anger him. But as I consider further their situation I can also see that she might have wanted to confide something so that, paradoxically, they would feel closer. Secrets separate, after all, and for her to disclose her arrangement with Abner to Jay could be a demonstration of intimacy. Her inner thoughts weren't any part of her deal with him. All Jay wanted was for her to behave in a certain way, do this and not do that, and be available. And her behavior had been irreproachable.

Bizarrely enough, it doesn't much matter which way we decide. Let us call it "cleaving," which can mean separating or binding together. (But rarely both.) She wrote Abner to tell him that Jay knew. To this she added, "And nothing has changed."

There is a point toward the end of *Wings of the Dove* where Old Hen loses me. Each one of his characters has figured out that the plan was for Merton to marry Milly so that, when she dies and he inherits her money, he can marry Kate and they can be together comfortably ever after. But when they are at last facing the truth, how do they behave? With Mr. James the general tendency is predictable. They will all demonstrate an incredible refinement that, in the end, James thinks is a function of their American "innocence," or, *bref,* stupidity. The reader is left to imagine what he or she would have done, behaving less well or better. And which is which? Merton's excessive delicacy messes everything up, but that's predictable, because the only thing James thought was more deplorable than sex was money. I think of the poor college kids, assigned the book, who read it dutifully, or the Cliffs Notes anyway, but when it comes to the essay they have to write what they convey is that they have no understanding of what's going on because they don't know anything about sex, money, love, or life. Their young brains are still too smooth.

So now Abner now knows that Jay knows. He writes to Nadine asking how and why. Has the plan changed? Not unreasonably, Abner would have been concerned that, with the pressure off, his relationship with Nadine would erode. Would she still want him? Need him? Indeed, would she even think about him? In daylight's banality, wraiths and spirits lose their power. It is a metaphor, of course, because our primitive fears recede when the sun rises but, more than that, the world returns to its everydayness, which may be less frightening but is also less interesting. Even Lubbock and Newport Beach turn real. Or as real as those places ever get. The rain birds wake up and make their graceful spirals on the lawns. It's another goddamn day and there is no choice but to try to get through it.

Which, for Abner, was horror enough.

What he didn't know and couldn't have imagined was Frannie's maneuvering. She came to the house from time to time so that he could go outside, walk around, go to the library, maybe, and enjoy the window displays of the Lubbock shopping area—for lack of anything else, he could admire the John Deere displays of tractors and cultivators—or more likely, ignoring what he saw, just walk around in the fresh air. He thought of these breaks as the exercise periods prison guards allow even to those in solitary confinement. They plod around in a circle in the yard, but there is blue sky overhead and, for that one hour in the day, they can feel the sun on their faces and can breathe.

Surely, it was a kind thing that Frannie was doing to allow him these moments of respite from their mother's incessant demands, a display of more consideration than he might have expected. Ah, but there's the difficulty. She resented him, had always compared her life with his and thought she'd been continually cheated. He got to go to Yale and then sashay around Europe and then hobnob in Hollywood with rich and glamorous people out there. She was the little brown hen they had kept in the coop in Lubbock. Their father couldn't bear to part with her and then, after he died, their mother insisted that she remain and not leave her all alone in the world. (There are phones, for God's sake, and airplanes. Yes, but that's not the same thing as you damned well know!)

But let us not get bogged down in reasons. Siblings often hate each other. For crazy reasons or none at all. He's seven, say, and she's four. Does he bully her a little? How could he not? She's younger and smaller, doesn't know anything, and resorts to wailing if she doesn't get her way. His birthday party was better than hers (or she thought so). Anything can be the seed of a resentment than grows over the years, as one thing after another seems to confirm the inherent unfairness of the younger one's lot. Cain and Abel? They were not just a one-off. Think of Esau and Jacob, Joseph and his brothers, and on and on. Schiller's "Ode to Joy" that Beethoven set to music was attractive because it was so unrealistic. If all men were brothers, we'd be even worse off than we are now.

In fact, that unrealistic ideal is a part of the problem. You're in the back seat and she kicks you. Not by accident, as you know she will claim, but on purpose. To elicit a kick or a punch in return, which can be an excuse for a howl of pain and an accusation that he hurt me. From the front seat there is disapproval and the repetition of the old nonsense about why can't you two just get along? For her, it's a tiny victory. For him, it's yet another affront for which he will try to get even when they are alone. And back and forth. Being older and larger, he wins most of these contests and she hates him for it. And she resents her parents for not interfering more often and more forcibly—obviously because they like him better, which is, of course, the main reason for her resentment. And she promises herself that one day, no matter how far in the future it may be, she will get even.

At last, Frannie sees her opportunity. She can right ancient wrongs and, for once, take control. The fact that she works for a law firm might have contributed to the mechanics of it, but the general idea had been there forever. She talks with her mother about what might happen if there were another stroke. What if she couldn't talk anymore? Does she really trust Abner to do the right thing, just out of the goodness of his heart?

Frannie's idea is that her mother should give her a power of attorney so she can write the checks and take care of the finances. And she suggests that her mother should set up a trust fund with Frannie as trustee so that she can dole out money a little at a time to keep Abner on a leash and here in Lubbock where he belongs, after all. And later, after Lurlene "passes," Frannie can conserve his share so that he doesn't go off and blow it on nightclubs and movie stars of whatever gender. Could they trust him? Could they rely on him? It's the right thing to do--for his sake even, although he surely won't see it that way.

That weird claim—that it would be for Abner's own good—is persuasive, not because the mother has ever had any evidence that the brother and sister are fond of each other but because she has always wanted them to be and that's the story she has told herself. Such fictions can be the engines of reality. A dear boy, he was, she had to admit, flighty, and Frannie's steadying hand would be a good thing. There was also the consideration that it wasn't her death they were preparing for (which she refused to think about) but her further disability, which she could almost bring herself to imagine. She was willing, therefore, to consider measures that might apply in either event.

It is easy enough to understand Frannie's silence. A part of the satisfaction she dreamed of was his surprise, the appalling moment of realization of how she had contrived to make him her dependent. We forget having been seven, but our bodies were there and our sense of ourselves was taking shape, more or less deformed by the strength of the prevailing winds that produce those picturesque, crippled trees on the Pacific coast. But the mother? Why was she so unforthcoming in all that time she and Abner were together? She had to have had her doubts about Frannie's plan, or Frannie's motives even. She might have had buyer's remorse. She certainly ought to have known that Abner would have objections that were not unreasonable. Perhaps she supposed that at some opportune moment, she would raise the question and they could discuss it together like civilized people. Or, more probably, she wanted to avoid the distress of yet another protracted fight with alternating periods of shouting and silence. She tucked that embarrassing notion away but could not help now and then remembering that it had crossed her mind.

He could have packed a suitcase and left. But that would mean he was abandoning his mother, which would also require some courage. To go to New York or Los Angeles, or even Dallas, to try to find work? He'd never had an actual job before. Be a book reviewer maybe? Lon Tinkle had that position sewed up at the *Dallas Morning News*. (Really! Once you've heard the name, you never forget it). A depressed person doesn't have the kind of courage and selfishness such an action would have required. What motivates the depressed to bestir themselves is usually blunt necessity. Then, too, Abner didn't actually need anything. He figured that when his mother died, Frannie wouldn't want him to stay around, so he'd be free, just as Nadine would be free when Jay died. A curious if grotesque symmetry. (Would he have confided this thought to Nadine?)

Day succeeded day, each of them filled with moments, but none opportune enough for Lurlene to begin a discussion with him about the trust arrangement. Talking was strenuous anyway. And her mood was terrible. The last thing in the world she wanted was a quarrel with her son that might drive him away. She didn't like having to depend on him, but there it was, a fact she had to face. Between Frannie and Abner, neither of whom she trusted altogether, she found herself trapped, and that idea was depressing. It was evidence of her failures as a parent. She tried to reason with herself. Maybe her doubts about her children were just an old woman's nervousness about everything. Her black mood could be the cause of her sense of failure as easily as it was the result. You don't know. You never know. It was frightening, as if she discovered one day that the walls of her room were not solid but just illusions through which she could poke her hand. Or just walk through them.

She knew that some of her fears were real. At any time, just going to the bathroom, she could slip, fall, hit her head on the edge of the tub, and die. These were not fanciful worries, and this recognition made them all the more frightening. Whether it was true or not, she took comfort in the thought that Abner could take care of himself. He could handle Frannie—as he had always managed to do. There was nothing to be gained by imagining the worst. She rolled over on her side, adjusted the pillows, and closed her eyes. If she was going to have nightmares, at least let them come when she was asleep.

She had signed the papers and somebody from the law firm had come with Frannie to witness them. Go through all that again? Admit that she had been taken for a ride? We are all being taken for a ride and most of the time we are in the back seat with no control over where we're going and nobody protecting us or even asking in annoyance why we can't just get along.

✳

I met the woman only once. One time for no more than five minutes, and many years ago. Because of her name and her aggressively artificial hair color, I thought of her, then and for years afterward, as a figure of fun, a character out of some mordant comedy that, if she had read it, she wouldn't have understood. She certainly wouldn't have liked it. But there it was, her life, in which she had been miscast. Also funny, right?

But if we think about her even for a little while, she changes, becomes more complicated, and even interesting if not quite attractive. The weirdest part of this is that I am, myself, convinced--not that everything is accurate but is plausible. The metadata are suggestive enough to restore those walls in her bedroom to solidity so that she can't just walk through them. We beguile ourselves. We're not trying to be just or charitable or responsible. We're not trying at all. The process happens. The scene assumes whatever details are necessary--Venetian shades in dusty rose and lampshades in the same color. Dove gray carpeting with an area rug beside the bed in some geometric Navaho pattern. Probably the rug is authentic.

I close my eyes. It doesn't help.

III

I take a liberty. Or, to be grandiose and continue in the authorial plural, we take a liberty. This delicate subject is quite far down the list of even the most tenderhearted humanitarian's concerns. We grant you that, right off. (You, here, being a putative audience, acquisition editors being most unlikely to have got this far in the manuscript.) We suggest, nevertheless, that writer's block is an interesting problem, not particularly poignant perhaps, but intellectually intriguing and morally complicated. The writer (he or she must have already established him or herself as a writer to qualify for membership in this gloomy club) just can't do it anymore. Okay. So what? The interesting aspect of this disability is whether it comes from humility and fear (I'm just not up to it; I know I shall disappoint myself; it will be so bad that I'll stop after ten or twenty pages and will feel even worse than I do now). Or is it, paradoxically, a symptom of pride? Can we imagine that there are lesser writers who are able to perform, because they don't have any expectations and are willing to settle for their best even if it isn't very good? They don't care about inevitable blows to their self-esteem (from inside and out) and they apply themselves in the undiscriminating selflessness of one of the mules in a wagon train.

These aren't questions one can ask of a blocked writer: does your problem arise from humility or pride? Well, you can ask, but only if your intention is to inflict further pain and to be insulting. We're not talking about talent or its lack but perseverance and psychic health, which are traditional enough concerns of novelists. (And the rest of us, too.) Call it character. There can be craftsmanly setbacks, but these are not fascinating. The writer realizes (usually about forty or fifty pages in) that it just isn't going to work. And he may be quite correct in this. (But not always. Dostoyevsky didn't figure out that Myshkin was a prince until the fourth draft of *The Idiot*.) There are a number of novelists and poets who seem to dry up but it is more accurate to say that they are allowing their critical faculty to overwhelm their creative impulse and to bully it into silence. From the readers' point of view, this can be a good thing, of course, but our concern here is with the psychodynamics of silence. The authorial idea of a manuscript is not authoritative, by which I mean merely that the pages may be much less good than he thinks or, on rare occasions, even better.

The point of this divagation, as you may perhaps have already guessed, is my effort to imagine and convey Abner's years in Lubbock, where, as his mother pointed out, there were tables, paper, pens, stamps, and mail boxes. If Flannery O'Connor could write in Milledgeville, Lubbock cannot be ruled out as a possible venue for composition. There are touching tales of writers in gulags who made their minuscule jottings on toilet paper or who, without any paper, composed their poems a line at a time, committing each new line to memory. For the sake of the poem? Or simply to keep from going mad. In Lubbock, Abner was warm and dry, well fed, able to shower and to listen to music. And his mother's taunts were true enough—there were paper, pens and ink.

He was thinking about it. I know this because there would sometimes be half-serious descriptions of projects he was considering. He was thinking of a version of *Tosca*, I remember, in which Tosca doesn't kill Scarpia but submits to him so that he spares Cavaradossi's life. (Or pretends to.) Much more interesting, and more likely for that matter. Without the music, the stabbing, shooting and detectation would be absurd (that last word, my invention, being the equivalent of defenestration if you throw yourself off a roof or *tectum*.) I have no idea how serious he was about this idea. I noticed, of course, that it had a certain connection to the trigonometry of his situation with Nadine and Jay, and this might have been a prompting for him to sit down and write out at least a few pages. When one gets involved in the making of sentences, the surround recedes and matters less and less.

Surely, his brain was working. Sometimes there would be lines he meant to put into something that he'd write in large majuscules in the margin at the top of a page: THE ATTITUDE OF A PLATYPUS IS A PLATITUDE, or IN A SAD ASIDE HE SAID THE AFFRONT TOOK HIM ABACK. He never explained these curious squibs, but I took them as signals to me and to himself that his brain was still working. Or they could have been challenges he'd set himself. Could he work such a line into a paragraph and have it sound natural? (For that matter, could I?)

I stare at the words of that second example, having just transcribed them. It is unlikely that that combination ever occurred before in English: he devised it, so it qualifies as a creation, a work of art, albeit a minor one. Is it complete, even if it poses as a fragment? Read it over again and you may take it as a biography in a single sentence. (Do I sentimentalize? Perhaps so, but the sentence is not at all sentimental and surely the text permits such an interpretation.) He was doing what writers do, playing with words as if they were Tarot cards that a random deal can sometimes arrange in a pattern that seems to tell us what we hadn't realized we knew. More modestly, one could take it as the warbling of a caged bird all of whose songs are sad.

✳

Our exchange of letters was intermittent, depending on whether we had anything to say. Or too much. Sometimes life can be too eventful to write about, just as it can be too tedious, in which case one is driven to invent stuff, which never feels right with an old friend. My point is that when months went by and I hadn't heard from Abner, I never worried about it. Who could say what was occupying him? Perhaps he was writing something else, a short story or a novel. More likely, he was just bored and depressed, which happens sometimes. Deeply depressed. He got out of bed later and later in the morning. What for? What was the point? It was ten o'clock for a while and then, later, closer to noon. And he also took naps in the afternoons, which were an excellent place to hide.

Lurlene had had another series of small strokes each of which further diminished her capacities. The four-footed cane went into the attic to be replaced by a walker. She got one of those fancy walkers that turn around to be a chair and have storage space under the seat, in gay fire-engine red. Those are for people who go out of the house, or at least can imagine doing so. She couldn't, but it was the best walker, which was, she thought, the least she deserved. She didn't speak much anymore but only pointed at what she wanted—her mouth if she was hungry or thirsty, or her backside if she needed to be taken to the bathroom. She had become an infant, the literal sense of which is not being able to talk. The caretaker took care of her, of course. Abner just came in to sit for a while in the afternoons, not even bothering to talk to her but just to be present, slouched in a chair, reading, and letting her look at him. After an hour or so of this, he'd go up to her, bend down to give her a kiss on the forehead, and go back to his room, done for the day.

He proposed to Frannie that they consider putting her in a home where she could get round-the-clock care from medical professionals. Frannie preferred things the way they were. Abner accused her of keeping him a prisoner in Lubbock. She laughed and asked him why he should have more freedom than she did. Back and forth, with more and more animus, until she reached the point where she told him about the trust, flung it in his face, and explained to him that essentially he was now her captive—unless, of course, he decided to get off his lazy ass and find a job, if there is a job out there for a ridiculous nutcase like you.

She told him the details of the trust arrangement and explained that she and the Cattleman's Bank were co-trustees. She also had their mother's power of attorney and would be handling all the finances. What this meant was that she was in charge of all the money and therefore of Abner, too. If he was a good boy, she'd let him have an allowance.

A joke, surely. This was crazy. She agreed that it might be crazy but that didn't mean it wasn't true. He looked into it and found out that it was real and, worse, that there was nothing he could do about it except scream at her that she was a vindictive little bitch, and that she was right about not having been loved when she was a girl because she was always a shitty little girl and had blossomed into a fat, shitty big, girl. He called her "swine-girl," an insult he had dreamed up when they were children that he knew she still hated. But now she just enjoyed it.

Hire a lawyer, maybe, to try to undo her mischief? With what money? She had it all. Kill her? The motive would be clear enough to point to him no matter how clever his plan, and anyway he didn't care enough to murder her. When Jay croaked, as he had to do eventually, Abner would be free of her. Until then, what he had to do was keep going, day to day and week to week, waiting to hear news from Nadine. But there had been an adjustment in his mental outlook and he had become broodier and even more depressed. Here in Lubbock there was a Gothic novel playing itself out. A silly idea, which if he thought about it the right way, could be funny. For a minute or two.

Some shrinks have persuaded themselves that exterior events don't cause depression. It's an illness, and its causes they say, are not in our scars but in ourselves. This is a convenient theory for them, because they can't do much to change external reality but they can treat patients and prescribe for them. (Their other tactic is just to change the label from depression to post-traumatic stress syndrome, which is a different malady and acknowledges the possible influence of the outside world. The medications are often the same.)

Abner didn't mention any of this to me, or to Nadine either, I'd imagine, because it wasn't interesting. Or, no, let's be honest. Because it was shameful. I've had my wallows and it never occurred to me to mention them to Abner or anyone else. You lie in bed, trying not to look at the clock with its heartless announcement that it's already ten o'clock. You get up to pee but then go back to square one, which is under the covers. You know where you are and what time it is, but you haven't altogether given in and turned on the television set. You don't have to make a total commitment, you tell yourself. You could get up and brush your teeth, but then you could reward yourself with a little rest from that exertion from those achievements. Because you are living on such a tiny scale, they count, each one, as an exploit. Sometimes, when you are more than usually delicate, the effort of swinging around and putting your feet on the floor is enough to signal that you are exhausted. "March or die!" you tell yourself. It is ludicrous but it has worked before, even though you don't particularly care about the legionnaires besieged in Fort Zinderneuf. They can go fuck themselves, as they probably do. You

allow yourself a few minutes more in sweet supinity. *Reculer pour mieux sauter.*
(You can perhaps *sauter* with orange peels.) Sometimes, you feel guilt about
your immobility, but that's because you are thinking of it as a character flaw
rather than a symptom. Never mind the disease, but in this very bed, when
he could talk his way into skipping school, he'd spend the day, drifting in and
out of sleep, with the blinds drawn, in a gloom he imagined as healing. Now,
too, in that same gloom in that same room. Not so complicated after all, the
myth of eternal return. The Odyssey of the Eliade.

His mother, he had to admit, was right. You're a writer and you have
a roof over your head, food, clothing, and nothing else to do but scribble.
You ought to be delighted. You could think of your confinement here as
an indefinite stay in a MacDowell Colony, but without anybody else in resi-
dence whose stupid conversations you have to endure and who are endlessly
inviting you to play tennis or go for long walks with them in the obsessively
manicured woods.

There is also the seductive thought that, until you get up and dressed,
you are unlikely to do anything wrong. If you were to manage to get to the
writing table with the silent accusation of those yellow pads and the pens,
you'd only write sentences that would immediately demand improvement.
Or, more likely, excision. Such efforts are invitations to failure. And having
tried and failed, you'd feel even worse than you did before you began.

In his stately indolence that Swinburne might have imagined, Abner
could propose projects to himself and then reject them. It got him nowhere,
but there was an illusion of working. What about that reworking of Tosca?
You complete five pages. Or three. And there'd be a sense of accomplish-
ment. You'd have earned your single malt. You could then relax in the evening, watch a movie or a baseball game, or listen to music and read and feel
okay about things. But take away the pages and you're a bum, a uselessness.
Work is impossible and even to imagine work is strenuous. If you were the
younger son of a belted earl, you'd have learned how to live this way. But
it takes years of training. Generations, even. Like those English lawns that
have to be rolled every day for two hundred years.

His mother had never redecorated his room, either because it wasn't
important (he wasn't living in it anymore) or because it was an exhibit of his
childhood into which she could peer sometimes to remember him as a small
boy—as people stare into Roosevelt's study at Hyde Park, which is just as he
left it and to which it seems he may return at any moment.

A cog slips in the machinery of time and he's back there with the same
wallpaper and the same light fixtures, having been demoted and sent back to
repeat those years like a slow kid redoing the fourth grade. Would he change
anything this time? (Change his name and go to Princeton?) It was painful
for Abner to look at the pictures of baseball players on the wall most all of

whom had long ago retired or died. The books on his shelves were also an irritation. Was he going to devote himself to a review of solid geometry? Of course not, even though it would have been a way to pass the time. (What prisoner in Eastern Europe wouldn't trade all his cigarettes for a solid geometry text? On the other hand, what consolation is there in the fact that others are worse off than and have suffered longer?)

Look Homeward, Angel. Yes, do that, and you'll be surprised to find that Thomas Wolfe was a terrible writer. Gushy and sentimental, as if he wrote in Marshmallow Fluff rather than ink. How could Abner not have noticed that back when he was assigned the book? Anyway, home is the place where, when you have to go there, they have to take you in, as Frost said and, even if he recognized the humiliation of it and the admission of abject failure, he was probably being optimistic.

On the plus side, though, while Abner's mother was having her strokelets, her transient ischemic attacks, Jay was experiencing "cardiac incidents,"--arrhythmias, for which there is treatment but no cure. Nadine continued to act (wasn't that what she had come out to LA to do?) as the good wife, but she also must have remembered at times the plan she and Abner had dreamed up. She would have to decide how serious Abner had been. Had it been just a joke? One couldn't always tell with him. He could have been fucking with her while he was fucking with her. If it was hard to see into his squirrely brain, it should have been easy (or easier) to answer for herself. Had she been serious? Or more to the point, was she interested now? The money wasn't going to be quite so abundant as they'd supposed. Jay's first wife and the trusts for his two kids came in for big pieces of the estate. But her share would allow them to live comfortably. If the possibility turned real, would she want that? She couldn't be sure.

Oddly, she had already reaped much of the benefit. Their pact was something she could think about during the long, sometimes tedious years of the marriage. Jay had been relatively undemanding sexually, but he was, as many of those moguls are, boring. Mainly he liked to put her on show at parties and award ceremonies. He read a lot. Books—in page proofs mostly—or screenplays and treatments. He would read in his study and then in the bedroom, and on vacations, he would read on the beach or, more likely, in the bar, which would be air-conditioned. Out on the sand, under a blue umbrella, Nadine could tell herself—and half believe it—that all this was an illusion, a transitory thing. But she was never taken in altogether. Life itself is transitory. This was as real as the blue-green sea, the puffy white clouds, and the fine-grained white sand. But then how real are they?

She kept from going crazy by thinking of Abner in that room he had described to her in one of his longer letters and how he was hanging on there by the skin of Thornton Wilder's teeth, thinking of her and how, eventually, they would be together again. At the very least, that consideration kept her from feeling that she was a fool. Or if she was, then they were fools together. As Abner had said, to reassure her, "Put enough lunatics together and they're not crazy anymore; they're a religion."

He had been trying to sound upbeat. Or not to admit how deep was his gloom. (Those last five words could be the title for a novel, although it would have to be a funny novel, ideally by Peter de Vries.) He could have let her know—but he didn't—that it seemed silly to get dressed just to go into his mother's bedroom and read there for an hour. So he lived in his pajamas and his bathrobe, like Hugh Heffner (who mostly dresses like some inmate on a ritzy mental ward, which is about right).

His connection with Nadine had been something to hold on to. Now, it was his hour of duty in Lurlene's room, each day a challenge (made all the more difficult because he wasn't sure if there was any point to it, whether it did her any good, or even whether she realized that he was there. Can you be an existentialist in Lubbock? He was. To prove what and to whom?

The end. Of course, it isn't, because you can see that there are still a few pages to the right of where you are (unless you're reading an e-book, in which case you have that line across the bottom of the page). But there's nothing in them. Trust me. The action stops here. Nothing else is going happens. The rest is persiflage. (Another possible line for Horatio to intone at the end of Hamlet.) The thing about dénouements in drama and fiction is that they are obvious fabrications, and while we'd love to believe in them most of us know better. All those misunderstandings cleared up and all the couples standing there ready to marry and live happily ever after? Life isn't a solitaire game in which, if you are patient, you can get it all to come out. *Noues* are not so easily or neatly untied. Patterns set up in the beginning of a book do not necessarily complete themselves in any significant way. In the vulgarity of the real world, we schlepp along as best we can and then we die. *Noue? Nu?* But who wants to read about such books or see such plays, even though we know they are true? It was, you will recall, ten of eleven when the book began. It's a quarter after four now, but the date has changed. That's all that happens. Tempus sure does fugit, don't it?

With Abner and Nadine, time passed, too. And things did happen, not necessarily as a result of their contrivances but certainly affecting them. For example, Nadine was driving her blue Beemer convertible, paying attention and wearing her seatbelt, doing all the right things, when the brakes on a large truck failed as it was coming toward the intersection from the left and hit the car broadside on the driver's side. Bang, just like that. No way of foreshadowing that kind of thing, is there? In French that would be *imprévu*, which is a perfume by Coty with a bergamot and bitter orange opening but then mildly leathery with the merest touch of cloves and fresh in that mossy way of classic chypres. (Pardon the unforeseen divagation but that's the name of the fragrance, isn't it?) What the name suggests is the splendid, mysterious lover who appears unexpectedly and sweeps the wearer off her feet, probably wearing an aftershave that has citrus notes on a base of oak moss.

What happened there? I was rattled a bit by the sounds of metal on metal and shivering glass and then, after a relatively brief pause, wailing sirens. I know I'm not involved, but it's still scary. They placed Nadine on an EMS stretcher and then on a gurney at the hospital. She had a broken pelvis, several broken ribs, and a shattered femur. She was in the hospital for several weeks and then at the rehab center for months more, learning first to use a walker and then taking a few baby-steps between the parallel bars with much bravery but not enough. (There's never enough.) There were further operations, none of which did what the orthopaedic surgeons promised or at least hoped for. Her frustration was such that even the most Buddhist patient would have broken into tears now and again.

Jay was the one who was supposed to die, perhaps in bed like John Garfield, the strenuousness of sex being too much for his heart. But *Der mentsh trakht un Got lakht*, which even people without German or Yiddish will be able to figure out easily enough. (Man plans and God laughs, but *plans* and *laughs* don't rhyme in English.)

Easy there. Don't get restless. You have a quarrel with how the universe is run? Take it up with God. Go and pray. Study Talmud. Or Aristotle or Buddha. Solid geometry, even. But don't blame me for being honest with you. That kind of thing generally passes for virtue in our post-lapsarian world. She wrote to Abner and, by this time, Jay knew enough about their bizarre scheme so that she could ask him to mail the letters. And bring her the replies. Which he was glad to do because they seemed to cheer her a little. He never read them but he had heard enough about Abner to be able to guess what they'd say—that he still loved her, was still waiting for her, wanted her to get well and, above all, not to lose hope. What the hell else could anyone say?

It is also possible that he felt a small, smug satisfaction that their lunatic plan had been ruined. Nadine was his, now, and even if she married Abner after he died, she wouldn't be the same woman anymore. Is that plausible? It's not something he'd have expressed aloud to anyone, but in his position (as an author one must imagine himself to be in his position) I'd probably indulge in some such ungenerous idea. It doesn't matter much, but it gives an interesting wrinkle to his mailing of Nadine's letters to the Texan. Or to revert to Old Hen, it makes for an all but undetectable defect in the lovely golden bowl of his generosity. (In a paragraph like this, I broach the idea without entirely endorsing it. It isn't cheating but actually honesty. What do I know, after all?)

They had both understood (or, more accurately, say that they had *each* understood) that things might go awry. What neither had guessed was that the more slender the thread that connected them, the more tightly each of them would clutch it. It seems paradoxical and perhaps too clever, but I think of missionaries in the jungle ministering to primitive tribes—medically, mostly, but also teaching and counseling. Their faith no longer burns with a bright, steady flame. Mostly, these fires burn themselves out in a matter of months, after which it takes an act of will to continue doing what they are doing. The will takes the place of the faith and is all the more praiseworthy for that. More valuable? I couldn't say--but I suspect not. Those first couple of years, Abner and Nadine's commitment to each other had been a pleasant conceit, a running joke. Now with Nadine crippled, it was more important. (I know that we're not supposed to say "crippled," but that's the word. "Handicapped" or "disabled" (or, worst of all "differently abled") are absurd euphemisms, which do not spare the feelings of the people they describe but rather those of the healthy people who are speaking of them and wish not to upset themselves. I may admit to being crippled, but "differently abled," never.) Derek Jeeter was differently abled, being a much better athlete than most of us.

On further reflection, never mind the missionary metaphor. Let us leave them to Evelyn Waugh and Graham Greene, who (almost) took them seriously. We can say without rhetorical figuration that this bright, attractive, but battered couple had decamped from the world in which I am typing this (and you are reading it) to the unreliable sanctuary of fiction's domain. Pretending to each other, they had become the characters in their congruent stories, which is pleasing (to me, anyway) because Abner was a novelist and Nadine was an actress. This is what such people are supposed to do, isn't it? The arbitrary constraints of space and time no longer operated for them. Intellection and emotion are mutable but they offered a refuge to which they could retreat and in which they could summon each other up out of the mists of memory and desire and, at least for a while, be where they wanted to be.

It's not what any of us might choose, I concede at once, but how often do we get to choose for ourselves? And there are advantages, as I believe Abner must eventually have realized. The main thing about a love affair in which the lovers never meet is its invulnerability. Or let them meet and then be separated forever. Tristan and Isolde or Abelard and Heloise cling to the idealized perfection of a snapshot. Vicissitudes of mood and lapses of courtesy cannot blemish such relationships, which therefore become ever more purified. Their love is not intellectual, but more modestly an idea of itself, what remains after time's refining fire. The imagined other is always there, continuously present and sympathetic. Abner could find solace in thinking of Nadine and could therefore assume that she found the same comfort in thinking about him. But then there were further complications, for as he imagined what she was thinking, he saw an image of himself, not a portrait from life but a representation of himself as a beloved lover. Dorian Gray in reverse, which is what happens unless we float off into the supernatural. More than the physical union, that abstraction is the heart of the heart of it. To be cared about, to be made to feel essential, and with a fervor that can be gauged by the level of his own, was a psychic luxury. It seems likely that his late risings and early retirings and the many naps in between were his strategy for being with her, elsewhere and otherwise.

Childish? Even infantile! Probably, but who is to say that the loves we felt in the sixth grade were not important? I know a number of relentless womanizers who have forgotten the names and faces of many of those they have bedded but recall vividly the girl in the aisle to the left and one desk ahead in the seventh grade who embodied a perfection for which they have been searching ever since. Stupid, perhaps, but intelligence has nothing to do with the case. The mind's wax is still soft when we are young and can take an impression, which soon hardens so that it remains for years as sharply incised as when it was new.

Abner's mother was too far gone to notice that there was anything wrong with her son. Frannie must have noticed but she was disinclined to offer him any help or even to suggest that he go out and find some. Indeed, she may have enjoyed watching his deterioration. I suppose it must have been one of his mother's caretakers then who saw that he was in even worse shape than the helpless old lady she had been hired to look after and who ventured to suggest, ever so diffidently, that she might think about his seeing a doctor. She probably wouldn't have suggested a "psychiatrist," which would have been presumptuous, but any doctor, taking the most cursory glance at him, would have known enough to refer him to a shrink without delay.

The opprobrium of our parents' time in regard to psychiatry has mostly receded, but there are a few of us left who worry about its possible connections to literature. Think of Oblomov, lying on his couch. Dr. Zhivago comes by (not Pasternak's Zhivago but, say, his great uncle, also a physician) to give him a bottle of pills, whereupon Ilya Ilyich feels much better, gets up from the sofa, and resumes a healthy life. Goncharov's novel is *kaput, nishto*. Or think of Cousin Pons, languishing in his bed, when Dr. Proust (Marcel's father and brother were both neurologists) pays him a visit and revives him.

He feels much better, although several months of M. Balzac's work is rendered nugatory. Perhaps more to the point, imagine a competent therapist coming to treat Gogol, or Dostoyevsky. Or Hart Crane. Or Berryman or Lowell. Different bodies of work entirely, or maybe none at all. Without their neuroses, phobias, manias, tics, and depressions, do they feel the need to waste time at a desk with a pile of manuscript increasing slowly on the right? Emily Dickinson was stark, staring mad. Marianne Moore slept with her mother until she (Marianne) was sixty years old. (The mind is an enchanting thing/ like a pterodactyl's wing…)

Other writers, however great or small their talents, wonder what will happen to them. Or whether, if the impulse to write should disappear, the bargain will prove to have been at least fair. There is at least the logical possibility that the writing will stop and the writer still won't feel a hell of a lot better. But depression is one thing and desperation, another, and it is the latter that prompts Abner to call the doctor who is taking care of his mother for a referral to a shrink. He gets two names and tries the first one who is at the Texas Tech Health Science Center. He makes an appointment. Almost heroically, he showers, shaves, and dresses. Even without the caretaker having specified, he had been able to figure out the general sense of her suggestion. (Lurlene's caretaker's name, if you care, is Jasmine Turnipseed, both of which are common enough names in the south even if seldom seen together in one startling confection, but I digress.)

I have no idea what meds they were using back them. It turns out to be beside the point anyway. Dr. Silliman is a responsible enough guy to insist that Abner have a general physical before he starts on any of the antidepressants or stimulants. Perfectly reasonable and correct. The internist wants a chest X-ray, which reveals a spot on Abner's lung. Not yet a death sentence. There are more tests and a CAT scan. But there are brain mets. And that is a death sentence.

This is not how these stories are supposed to go! It's the girl who dies, as in *Love Story* or *La Bohème* or *La Traviata*. The guy is supposed to be left heartbroken but otherwise in excellent health, treasuring the bittersweet memory and so forth. For the man to die is a violation of the entire genre. Still, it happens, as we perfectly well know. Actually, men die on average sooner than women.

Needless to point out, Abner's depression is not much relieved by this news.

IV

Pretend that these are real people. I couldn't possibly comment except perhaps to observe that this is exactly what most readers do when they read fiction. Some of them search for Proust's models, motivated by their unease in the face of mere invention. How much of the Duc de Guermantes did the author imagine and how much did he take from Comte Henri Greffulhe? Is anyone reassured to learn that Comte Robert de Montesquiou may have been the source of some of the traits of the Baron de Charlus? How much of Charles Ephrussi is in Swann?

These are not interesting questions. If the scholars had all the answers to them, they still couldn't sit down and write a novel like Proust's. What they think they might learn from is the difference between the truth and the fiction, as if one could distinguish. The paradox of the parallax? Corrected manuscripts don't give any clue either. I don't care what he drew on to make his characters, who in the book are as real as they need to be. But here we have a more complicated problem. What if our characters, notionally real, decide, themselves, to become fictions? There must be books in which something like that happens, but I can't think of one.

The letters back and forth continue, but they are from and to increasingly fictive people. Abner makes no mention of his cancer. (What for? It would upset her—or at least he assumes it would. He hadn't told her about his depression and he didn't tell her about this, either.) And as I discovered only later she never specified the extent of her disability. How could Abner have been in love with an ideal woman who, after a series of medical catastrophes, wound up with only one leg? Each of them constructs an alternate and more attractive reality with pen in hand, better than the disagreeable randomness in which they find themselves. An actress (sort of) and a novelist (or former novelist) collaborate in an artifact. Improvised theater, but without an audience, which, if they had one, would only taint their efforts. They both understand that no producer will touch it without drastic revision.

What else is love—anybody's love—but a mutual deception, a folie à deux that manages at least for a while to dismiss reality as unsatisfactory and irrelevant? In this instance, the fantasies were collaborative, each taking cues from the other. Both he and she knew that their outgoing letters were figments, but each assumed nevertheless that the incoming ones were real. (This is the opposite, a cynic might suggest, of prayer.)

I have just reread the foregoing and, while it's roughly true, we can smooth it out a bit by changing "deception" into "courtesy." Courtliness. Nobody uses the term anymore but it used to be said of young couples that they were "courting," which should imply at the very least a studied, reciprocal politeness. Men and women in a relationship have to learn at least when to keep their mouths closed. (This would have been an excellent idea for James' characters but, for all their delicacy and refinement, Milly, Merton, and Kate turn out to be deplorable, magnificent, and all but unbearable blabbermouths. And, even worse, clumsy. Which is maybe the joke of that novel. It's a comedy but also a test, because those of us who are shrewd enough or mature enough are unlikely to be lulled into an inappropriate admiration for what the dopey characters, for all their pretentions to refinement, do and say. The hard question is whether this is what James intended. Is the whole thing tongue-in-cheek? One could argue either way.)

It follows, I am sad to say, that this, too, is a comic novel, as I could not have suspected when I began. Disappointments are comedies, aren't they, and failures of all kinds? Balzac was the master of this genre in his *Comédie humaine*, which isn't at all a thigh-slapper but is comedic if you are tough enough to see it. The characters may not be smiling, but readers, observing their want of self-awareness, are invited to. Chaplin's little tramp is seldom merry, but his audiences can hardly catch their breath from laughing. Tears are running down their cheeks, sometimes tears of one kind and sometimes of another. Both kinds are real.

It took me a while to realize this about James' novel. I was in the bluebird reading group in the second grade (we were the best in the class) but no one told us that we would have to grow up in order to understand what we were reading—Proust, Joyce, Balzac, or anyone else. It also took me a long time even to come to a glimmer of understanding about Abner, but that was because I lacked essential information. Then, at about this time, I got a long letter from him, longer than usual, in which he broke the news to me that he was dying. No, he didn't want me to come to Lubbock. Indeed, he wanted me not to come. What would we accomplish? We'd spend an hour or two together, and I'd go back to the real world, which would cost a lot and take much more time than the visit itself. Also he didn't want to burden me. He said he looked like shit and, while he wasn't especially vain, neither was he enthusiastic about my seeing him in such a condition.

As far as I could tell, he wasn't particularly upset by the prospect of dying. He'd been heading in the direction of disappearance for years. Forever. (Haven't we all?) If you think about it in a certain way, he observed, death is what makes human lives important. The Olympian gods live forever, so that whatever they do, both good and bad, is trivial. Our behavior is more important because it defines us. It counts.

I was considering this surprising display of Epicureanism when I came to the even greater surprise, which was that he hadn't told Nadine and wasn't planning to. He had written a letter for her that the nurses had promised to mail after he died, and in it he had explained that it was his love for her that had kept him from delivering this news beforehand. It had been his preference to pretend with her that nothing was wrong. They had been pretending for years, and why on earth stop now? With whom else could he contrive in any sense to be among the living? He had written to a few of his friends, from whom he could get all the sympathy or sadness or pity he could use. With her, he wanted to hold on to the dream of a future—and hope that it was a vivid dream.

Aside from the terrible news about his terminal disease, what struck me most about the letter was Abner's explanation of why he was keeping Nadine in the dark: "I can't be sure of this (who in this life can be sure of anything?) But I am free to suppose that Nadine has been less than perfectly happy in her marriage. This doesn't mean that it's a bad marriage, but any couple will experience some friction over the course of time. And she has kept up the correspondence, so I assume that I have been useful to her. Or the thought of me has been useful. I am happy to have been of any help to her, even the most trivial and ridiculous. It would be ignoble of me to abandon her. And if I told her now, I should feel that I'd betrayed her and myself, too. I need to think of her reading my letters and thinking of me as I used to be. For her, I haven't changed at all. I'm not in a hospice bed but driving along the Pacific Coast Highway in a silly Hawaiian shirt and sunglasses, without a care in the world. And in our imaginations she can be next to me. It's a convertible, although we were never in a convertible together. Fire-engine red. And the wind is plucking at the stray strands of hair it has managed to free from the confinement of her scarf. Hermès of course. Or to put it another way, it's a gift and I'd be an idiot not to let her keep it and take comfort from it. You're one of the few people I can tell about this."

What was I to make of that? I can't say that I approved, although, in part I did. I couldn't simply dismiss it as just another example of Abner's wackiness. It made enough of an impression so that I kept thinking about it and trying to puzzle out some meaning, or at least a resolution of my uncertainty. He died about a month later, and a few of his old college friends exchanged letters and phone calls, condoling with one another. As he had intended that we should do. I looked at his obituary in the *Avalanche* and discovered that all of us, the entire Yale class, were honorary pallbearers. I'd never been notified. None of us had been. It was in the obituary notice, though, so that anyone who bothered to look it up would discover this information. And the rest of us—the rest of them—didn't matter. Quirky? But then he'd had a lot of time to think about "arrangements." His mother survived him, although I shouldn't imagine that it was for very long.

This is a novel, right? I can do any damned thing I want. Let Abner find some curious "healer" in the mountains of Belize who, with coffee enemas and a strict diet of Brussels sprouts and pomegranate juice manages to bring about a remission or even a cure. Let him be carried off by a big bird to a Bhutanese dzong where the monks spin prayer wheels for him, day and night. Too stupid? But there's a drama, isn't there, of intelligent people, desperate enough to believe the most arrant nonsense. Think of Steve McQueen, who wasn't a dope but went down to find some persuasive charlatan and waste money on his therapy that he might have spent more sensibly on horses, whiskey, and women. Abner was smarter than McQueen, and probably less desperate. Death, itself, is not a tragedy, although it often punctuates tragedies. It happens. If your life has been terrific, you look back on it in gratitude. And if it has been mostly disappointing or painful, you don't mind letting go of it. We never talked about these things in our letters, which makes them, too, fictional. We were trying to cheer each other up and carefully avoiding the dead elephant in the room. I colluded in that and am sorry. I could have been more helpful, I think, if I hadn't been so tactful--out of stupidity and cowardice more than good manners.

He's dead, poor old Bitsy. And having something to blame myself for, I think of him often, which is the best the dead can expect of us.

A couple of years later, Jay Bishop died. Of a heart attack. Just as he was supposed to do. His widow, Nadine, wasn't rich but apparently more than comfortable. Except for Abner's cancer and Nadine's accident, the daffy plan could have worked. In a way, it represented what we are all taught about postponing present rewards in the hope of getting better ones after the passage of time. Very middle-class, actually, although that was never the way I thought of Abner.

Write about him? I thought of it briefly and then dismissed the idea. Not while Nadine was still alive. These were her secrets, too, and I had no right to broadcast to the world what Abner had communicated to me privately. But beyond that, there was my reluctance to write about a friend because even the notion of doing so made me realize how little we knew each other. And while I could fabricate, I would feel uncomfortable about traducing reality that way—assuming that there is such a thing. Even for a writer, there can be a private life. If I'd learned anything from Abner, that was the most striking lesson. On the other hand, his was the first life I'd watched from that day his parents dropped him off at Taylor Hall to its untimely end in Lubbock. To have seen the whole arc of it was impressive, even intimidating. What did it mean? Do any of our lives have "meaning," or even a general direction? How much control do we have even of that?

When your parents die, no matter what the relationship may have been, you feel exposed. Unprotected. You're an orphan and you're next. It's not a catastrophe. (What else could you have expected, after all?) But it makes you think. As does the death of a close friend of longstanding. It that all there is to it? What did it amount to? What does my own life amount to?

These are not questions that come up often. But they're always there and now and again obtrude themselves, leaving you speechless and breathless because there are no answers.

Eight or nine years after that, Nadine died. At last, I had the information I needed now to understand them (a grand claim) but at least to hazard a plausible guess about their relationship. Her obituaries were generally brief, noting that she had appeared in a few films, had married Jay Bishop, and then, after his death, had worked as a volunteer in a clinic in Kisoro in Uganda. This was hardly what I would have expected. She visited Africa twice a year, which was strenuous for a woman with a prosthetic leg who needed a crutch to get around.

I wondered whether any doubt had ever crossed Abner's mind. Or Nadine's. My guess is that neither of them could have afforded doubt because their shared pretense was central to both their lives. I supposed that she had regrets about Jay, about Abner, and about her own life. Her secular missionary work? It was either a search for worth or else some kind of penance. There is nothing in what I've been able to read about her to suggest that she was church-y. But that doesn't mean she didn't have a spiritual side. And spending money on a shrink is self-indulgent compared to devoting one's time and energy--and money too—to good works. Why Uganda? There is plenty of suffering in East LA, but Uganda is more dramatic. A lot of the movie stars make hobbies of Africa, adopting families or whole villages for which they can be fairy godmothers and fathers. Some of them get bored fairly quickly. (It isn't very interesting work after the first few months, however useful it may be.) Others keep at it, perhaps having gone native enough to expect that they will acquire the good juju that comes from the performance of good deeds. However I explain it, I am glad that she was mysterious and complicated enough to puzzle me. Puzzlement is not a bad place to come out. But I do admire her and, of course, Abner, too

During recent months Abner has changed for me, as the dead are liable to do. He is no longer a mere has-been novelist but a romantic hero. He is for me, anyway. To have experienced such a singular love? How rarely does that happen in our relentlessly pedestrian age? Whatever you think of them, you have to grant them a degree of originality, which is difficult to achieve. Originality is what writers aim for. I realized that I envy him.

I also thought of Petrarch and his Laura. (Did you know that "Laura" means "breeze" and suggested to him that any slight movement of air on his cheek he could take as a metaphor for her touch? I thought, too, of Dante and Beatrice and how *La Vita Nuova* is one long love letter. But mostly I thought of Heloise in her convent at Argenteuil and Abelard in a monastery writing letters that are now legendary. Everybody knows about his having been castrated by the angry mob, which is an excessively dramatic feature of the story. But not everyone is aware of what the letters said. Over and over, Peter Abelard kept insisting that he'd never loved her and that all he'd ever felt toward her was carnal desire. What is poignant about this and makes it memorable is that he was almost certainly lying in an effort to help her stop loving him so that she might be in less pain. And the only reason for his doing this was because he loved her. Exquisite, no?

Even more refined, however, is a correspondence in which both parties are lying or at least omitting essential information. It is a silence that each maintained for the other's sake. And it is through this resonant silence that their love expresses itself.

With Abner and Nadine, was it love? What else could it have been?

OTHER ANAPHORA LITERARY PRESS TITLES

Film Theory and Modern Art
Editor: Anna Faktorovich

Interview with Larry Niven
Editor: Anna Faktorovich

Dragonflies in the Cowburbs
Donelle Dreese

Domestic Subversive
Roberta Salper

Radical Agrarian Economics
Anna Faktorovich

Fajitas and Beer Convention
Roger Rodriguez

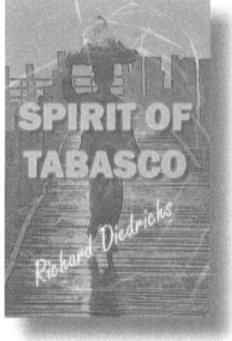

Spirit of Tabasco
Richard Diedrichs

Skating in Concord
Jean LeBlanc